MW00535305

Killer Review

The Painted Lady Inn Mysteries

By

M. K. Scott

Published by The Sleeping Dragon Press

Copyright © 2016 M. K. Scott
Print Edition

To obtain permission to excerpt portions of the text, please contact the author.

All characters in this book are fiction and figments of the author's imagination.

Chapter One

J.E. MUSCOVY COULD destroy a restaurant and kill a chef's career with a mere sentence or two in one of her cutthroat reviews. The acerbic summations not only appeared in the top papers, but were also available online and with a phone app. Former popular eateries' clientele would thin out almost to the point of nonexistence after a visit from J.E.

On the other hand, a career could experience a major boost if J.E. deemed a restaurant as good, even to the point of praising particular dishes. Those in the food world whispered a good review from J.E. always preceded a Michelin star, the gold standard in the culinary world. No wonder chefs longed for and feared a visit from the mercurial reviewer.

Donna stared at the laptop. She blinked, but it was still there. Daniel touched her shoulder as he went by, but instead of addressing her, he called out to his wife.

"Maria, I think a pod person has taken my sister's place. All she does is stare at the computer screen in total silence."

Her sister-in-law's tinkling laughter irritated Donna. Didn't anyone realize how serious this was?

"I think she's in shock. Her idol may have booked a room."

While she usually enjoyed Muscovy's no-holds-barred reviews, she'd never been at the possible receiving end of one. Janice, a nurse turned chef, alerted her to the reviewer's visit. Somehow, the woman knew everything in the food world, even when the health inspector would arrive. Thankfully, she tipped off Donna before the recent arrival of said inspector. Even knew what the target focus would be, which happened to be pantries and fridges last time around.

Janice's colorful bistro, The Croaking Frog, might merit a visit from the illustrious reviewer. Even though it didn't boast the label of fine dining, it had appeared on *The Food Channel* as a hidden gem. The locals who kept the place in the red during the lean years found it harder to get in after that with the influx of so many foodies checking out the place.

Legacy had become a hot spot for food tourists since not one, but two fine dining restaurants decided to locate here. Sylvester's Salon was a pretentious place with waiters who could out-snob the queen. Despite the inflated prices, an entrée didn't provide enough food to feed a toddler. Janice joked in the beginning that most of her customers came directly from Sylvester's to her place since they hadn't received enough to eat.

Sylvester's competition came in the form of Norelle's, an upscale Cajun restaurant. The words upscale and Cajun should have been an oxymoron when put together, but it wasn't. The interior was kitschy with dark touches such as the grinning crystal skulls at the bar to remind people even good times were temporary. Norelle's prices were as high as Sylvester's, but the portions were significantly larger, which created a strong customer base.

Another morbid draw was the wall of death. It didn't apply to anyone who managed to consume a thirty-two ounce porterhouse steak in one sitting. Oh no, Norelle's was much worse. Near a dark corner, the wall took an odd swing as if someone had tried to build a secret alcove but wasn't too covert about it. On the short wall were black-and-white photos of celebrities and dignitaries, dead ones. The popular establishment had started in New Orleans so those pictured could have visited the restaurant once, but Donna didn't think so. All she knew was a new photo went up a day or two *before* someone died. They always died, which was creepy. It also kept her from examining the wall too closely, just in case her photo showed up.

A cup of coffee appeared near the laptop along with her brother pulling up a stool to the kitchen island. "Give it a break. You don't know that the Jane Ellen Muscovy who booked online is your mysterious poison pen reviewer."

She shot her brother a look of disbelief. "Janice confirmed it. You know she has moles everywhere."

Maria balanced a stack of empty snack baskets on her hip as she strolled by and added her two cents. "If Janice Cunningham tells you something, believe it. That woman could run a crime family or a spy organization single-handedly. I'm not sure she doesn't. She probably tells the staff at Norelle's who will die next."

Daniel snorted. "Please. Have you all gone crazy? One solitary woman picked the inn to stay at, and the two of you start weaving tales."

Men sometimes couldn't see what was right in front of them. "Solitary single woman, that's it. It would be different if she had a companion. Then it might be a vacation. If I had a bunch of single women, then it would be a girls' weekend. Make a note, we should offer girls' weekends. Maria, what should we offer for the girls' weekend?"

"Mmm." Her sister-in-law hesitated before answering as she arranged brownies, cookies, and individual-sized snack bags of chips and crackers in the baskets. "Wine, discounts at the local spa, maybe a free gift. Perhaps you could get Janice to throw in a buy-one get-one meal free coupon?"

The back door swung open letting in the cool autumn air as Tennyson entered with her dog, Jasper. Donna held up her hand to her live-in helper. While the boy worked practically for free, any attempt at conversation resulted in a long existential discussion about the meaning of life. What did she expect from a philosophy major?

He wasn't her first choice for the job with his mournful expression, as if his soul hurt along with his feet. Truthfully, he was her only candidate. A tiny bedroom, a pocket-sized bathroom that doubled as a laundry room, free Wi-Fi, and two meals a day along with sixty dollars a week wasn't the lure Daniel thought it would be.

Tennyson had the nerve to complain about her cable package. She'd almost given the kid the boot before he even started, but Jasper liked him. Dogs were supposed to be good judges of character, but it was hard to remember someone Jasper didn't like.

Her brother greeted Tennyson. "How's it hanging?"

Really. That would be the nail in her B and B coffin if J.E. were here. She had once devoted a paragraph about a restaurant where the coat check girl and hostess had debated the paternity of a child. The place, instead of getting a star, got a V for vulgar.

A long sigh answered his query. Good. She didn't have time for a soliloquy on the deplorable state of humanity or some circular logic about a man only thinking he existed, but didn't in reality. The bluebird of unhappiness would arrive anytime.

"I better recheck all the rooms."

She'd moved Jane Ellen into the best room. Why she even went to the trouble to select the room mystified Donna since she spent more time removing her stuff as opposed to actually using the ground floor room while the inn had guests.

Her brother's voice stopped her before she hit the swinging door to the foyer.

"Your mysterious single woman could just be here to conduct an illicit affair with a married man."

Her eyes rolled upward. Daniel thought that was the bright side. She used her key to give her room one final check. The fresh flower arrangement she'd asked Maria to pick up looked good, except for the lilies and carnations. She plucked out the two small lilies and the three carnations. A careful relocation of the greenery hid any holes the plucked flowers might have caused.

The offensive flowers she'd hide in the outside dumpster. Carnations and lilies reminded her of funerals. The last thing she needed at the inn was anything that smacked of death. She cradled the rejected flowers in the crook of one arm, rather like a beauty contest winner.

Voices in the hall alerted her that some of her guests had already arrived. An unfamiliar woman's voice twined with Daniel's. Maria stood behind the table typing in the needed information. Tennyson slid into the room sporting a shirt that read "Kill Yourself Now and Spare Yourself the Pain".

Donna's eyes almost popped out. *Where did that come from?* Under the guise of being helpful, she'd offered to do Tennyson's laundry and deep-sixed most of his shirts. She'd replaced them with similar plain T-shirts, hoping he might think the depressing messages vanished in the high-heat dryer. He'd never said anything, but then he went out and bought more. In the dictionary, there had to be a snapshot of Tennyson next to the passive-aggressive definition.

Of course, the middle-aged woman dressed all in black might not be the critic. She could be here for a mortuary conference or a reunion for aging Goths. Everyone knew New Yorkers always wore black, at least that's what Janice said. It was easy to pick them out even in the sultry summer months due to their dark garments. It was almost like a uniform so they could identify one another in an emergency.

Her rapid gait almost approached a jog but not quite. Donna pasted a smile on her face while cutting her eyes to Tennyson, warning him not to move. He might offer to carry the woman's luggage as she'd prompted him to do before, even hinting he might get a tip for his trouble. The last thing she needed today was Jane Ellen looking at his T-shirt and giving the inn an A as in places to Avoid. The reviewer was big on using letter designations. All J.E would have to do is mention her dissatisfaction to a bed and breakfast reviewer which would automatically prejudice any future reviews. As a bigwig reviewer, the lesser reviewers would try to toady up to J.E., which could hurt The Painted Lady Inn. Tennyson's eyebrows drew together in confusion, confirming he'd received her message, and he stepped back into the kitchen.

"Welcome to The Painted Lady Inn," she said with enthusiasm, causing everyone to look her way.

Her brother wiggled his eyebrows. The woman's unsmiling countenance suggested she was indeed the critic. A judgmental glance started at Donna's head and swept downward to her toes. Donna wondered if any food was on her face. Maybe her hair was sticking up from checking under the beds. After a lengthy silence, the woman smiled.

"You brought me flowers. How nice. Lilies and carnations, my favorites."

Donna had no choice but to give her the offensive flowers as if that had been her original intention. No surprise, blooms normally seen at funeral homes would suit the critic. Perhaps she threw a carnation on the smoking wreckage of a dream she had just destroyed. "I could put them in an arrangement in your room, if you'd like."

"Ah, yes, I would like that. A small glass of your best sherry would suit, too."

Maria held up the room key, her eyes flicking between Donna and Daniel. Her brother grasped the key and swept up the suitcase, leading the parade to the room. Jane Ellen followed Daniel.

"How long has your inn been in operation?"

Daniel threw a grin over his shoulder. The same expression had melted more than one feminine heart before his marriage. "Oh, almost a year now."

"Really?" The woman angled her head, taking in the stairs and an ornate painting in the hall that depicted a Victorian woman and her two children in a garden setting. She gestured to the image. "Is the family part of the inn's history?"

Her brother, who never had a clue where the various items came from, didn't answer immediately. Perhaps he was debating about revealing the inn's checkered past, including its stint as a VFW and a destination for murder.

Donna moved a step closer. "It could be the original owner's wife. The general story is he built the house as a labor of love for his new wife." Actually, Herman had revealed the place was a showy piece of architecture built to display the man's prestige.

"That's a lovely story, but probably made up by the real estate agent to sell the place."

Well, it was a bit of creative fiction on her part. The critic had that much right. Jane Ellen's plain speaking appealed to Donna. Perhaps, Janice exaggerated the woman's negative impact on businesses. Surely, people would realize her review was one person's opinion. Would everyone quit going to a restaurant because the topping on the crème brulee wasn't crispy enough to suit one individual?

She remembered that a scathing review of the inn citing how one of her second-floor bedrooms was so pink it irritated, had future visitors requesting not to have the pink room. Yeah, she could see why Janice feared the woman's visit.

The woman might decide to write a review on The Painted Lady Inn. With that in mind, she'd have to do backflips to keep her happy. She poked the flowers back into the arrangement while Daniel explained the breakfast times. "We'd be happy to bring breakfast to your room."

The woman waved them both away. "My body is a temple. Now, where's my sherry?"

Yeah, a temple. Donna hot-footed it out of the room before she said something out loud. The only sherry in the house was cooking sherry. She'd have to stop Maria before she poured it into an aperitif glass.

No sign of her sister-in-law in the kitchen, although Tennyson stared at a half-filled glass of water. He called it contemplation. She snorted when he'd previously explained he received sympathetic vibrations from the liquid.

"Tennyson, where's Maria?"

The college junior jerked. His hand slipped on its perch on the island, causing him to contemplate the water much closer before he stopped his descent with his other hand. Exactly as she thought. He'd mastered the elusive art of sleeping with his eyes open.

He blinked twice, confirming her initial thought. "Whadya say?"

"Maria. Where is she?"

The young man's brow furrowed as if trying to analyze her

words for some hidden meaning. She was about to restate the question when the back door opened. A breathless Maria rushed into the kitchen, clutching an ornate glass bottle in one hand.

"I found some. Herman keeps some quality sherry to impress the ladies. I remembered him saying that once."

Donna blew out a breath. Someone paid attention to her elderly neighbor Herman's various stories. Though not a sherry fan, she could remember small glasses were part of the serving since it was more potent than regular wine.

"Thank goodness. I don't know anything about sherry except little old ladies drank it in the old black-and-white movies. Get online and see if we are supposed to serve something with it, like wafers."

Her sister-in-law chuckled as she reached for the laptop stored in the cabinet. "It's not communion. I never heard of it served with anything." The sound of light finger tapping replaced her words.

Donna rolled the bottle in her hand in an effort to find a bottling stamp that would clue her to the age of the beverage. No doubt the critic waiting impatiently for her drink would know in one sip.

"Uh-oh." Maria glanced up from the computer. "We have a problem."

Having a cutthroat critic in her inn wasn't enough of a problem? Donna inhaled, closed her eyes, and mentally counted to ten. The action was supposed to calm her. She opened her eyes and nodded for what had to be unwelcome information.

Maria turned the laptop screen in her direction. There was a long list of varying temperatures for sherry to be served depending on its specific type. In the end, the liquor had to be chilled and the bottle in her hand was room temperature. "We're screwed."

"It's in metric, too. Who can figure all this stuff out?"

Tennyson leaned over to look at the screen. "I can read it. What type of sherry do you have?"

Her woebegone helper could speak in something other than rhetorical expressions. He could also interpret metric, which was never a skill she even considered useful until now. She held the bottle up to the light to better read the label. "It's a dry Amontillado."

"That's thirteen in Celsius, which would be about fifty-six degrees." Tennyson grinned as he delivered the information. "That means it is only slightly lower than room temperature. All you need to do is wrap a wet paper towel around it and put it in the freezer for a few minutes."

Her surprise at this stranger who had taken over her helper's body kept her silent, but not Maria.

"Isn't Amontillado the wine in the Edgar Allan Poe story?"

It probably wasn't something she needed to know. If a damp paper towel cooled down a bottle fast, she'd use a dishtowel. That had to be faster.

Maria and Tennyson chattered about the story that had a man bricked up in a wall as she placed the wine in the freezer. How long should she leave it? Wouldn't J.E. be looking for it? The fact her brother hadn't returned meant he was busy turning on the charm. Daniel taught her one thing. Women responded favorably when a handsome man chatted them up.

The door swung open, revealing her red-faced brother. "Where's the sherry? That woman was quizzing me on the inn and made some derogatory sounds when I didn't answer the questions to her satisfaction. I felt like I was back in Sister Mary Elizabeth's class. I'm surprised she didn't whip a ruler out of her suitcase to slap my hands for unsatisfactory conduct."

Donna met Maria's surprised gaze. Daniel's charm was legendary—until now.

"Pour her a huge snifter," Daniel encouraged. "You might want to throw her some raw meat, too."

A quick pivot allowed Donna to hide a smile. Her brother had just met a female who hadn't hung on his every word. Sure, it was petty of her, but sometimes she just wanted her brother to live in the same world as everyone else. A quick detour to the large utility drawer would net the food thermometer. At least it measured in both Fahrenheit and Celsius. The space where she kept it in the metal organizer was empty.

"My thermometer is missing." *Great Scott, what else could happen?*

Daniel and Maria looked at her in confusion, probably not realizing why she needed the thermometer. Tennyson, on the other hand, looked away, reminding her of Jasper when caught sleeping on the furniture.

"Have you seen it, Tennyson?"

He pulled it slowly out of his pocket. No wonder he could figure out the temp conversion so fast. Instead of being upset, his ingenuity impressed her.

"Did I ever tell you that you have excellent critical thinking skills?"

He shook his head slowly and held out the thermometer. Donna shook it, hoping to bring the temperature down, and then ran it through water to clean it before using it on the wine.

She poured it into an elegant tulip glass with a short stem. The thick liquid measured an amazing 57 degrees. "If we hurry, we can get it to her before it gets warmer." She glanced around hopefully only to see the three of them looking away.

"Cowards." She placed a paper doily on a small tray and the glass on it. She carried the tray on her fingertips reminiscent of a train waiter she'd spotted on a family vacation. He had told her his fingers could counterbalance the motion of the locomotive. With any luck, she could counteract the venomousness of the woman. Too bad she had no clue how to do that.

The door swung open, revealing a woman who acted as if she'd just stepped into something nasty. "I only have two feather pillows and two of those horrible foam pillows. I will need two extra pillows—feather." She uttered the last word louder as if Donna couldn't figure it out on her own.

"I'm on it." She handed the woman the tray without the benefit of any ceremony. Thank goodness she had spare feather pillows in the linen closets. Most visitors preferred the foam.

After plumping the pillows into starched pillowcases, she headed back downstairs to deliver them. Reluctant to deal with the woman again in under ten minutes, she waited at the guest room door, hoping the sherry might have mellowed her out. The woman's voice carried through the door, proving the rooms were far from sound-proof.

"Yes, I know it's never personal."

She must be on the phone. The woman wouldn't appreciate her knocking and interrupting her phone conversation. A pause indicated the other party was talking, unless J. E. had hung up the phone without the benefit of saying goodbye. She waited just to be sure, qualifying it as politeness and not eavesdropping.

The strident tone had softened into resignation. "Ah, yes, but we used to be friends, close friends. You know what I mean… Okay… Will do." A heavy sigh penetrated through the bedroom door.

Afraid the woman might swing open the door and find her listening, Donna knocked. Something like that would definitely go into a bad review, too. The door swung open, but a wearier woman had replaced the one who'd checked in. J.E. didn't say a word. She grabbed the pillows and shut the door.

The overheard conversation had almost made Donna feel sorry for her, but the woman's lack of manners wiped that impulse firmly away.

The bell jingling, along with the front door closing, echoed down the hallway. More guests she needed to check in. Instead, Felicity, one of her neighbors, waited in the hallway. The well-preserved, blonde-haired woman held a lavender envelope. She lifted her hand in a wave, wiggling her fingers slightly. "Hi, Donna."

The fact Felicity used her first name caused her to miss a step as she strolled toward her. "Hello, Felicity. What can I do for you?" She knew good and well the woman wouldn't be booking a room.

Felicity met her eyes, tried for a smile that didn't bother to inform the rest of her face of her intentions. The result resembled a baring of teeth as she held out the envelope. "I have an invitation for you to the book club."

What? Donna forced her expression to remain neutral as she took the proffered invite. She turned it over and ran her thumb against the embossed seal. It was practically the equivalent of having tea with the queen. She'd been a part of the neighborhood for almost eighteen months and never before received an invitation to anything.

Her detective friend, Mark Taber, informed her that none of the families was as well placed or as moneyed as they liked to pretend. He recommended she forget about their afternoon teas and book groups and even told her she was better off without them. It didn't stop her from wanting an official welcome, though.

Felicity backed away once she delivered the envelope, but her gaze climbed the walls, even peeked into the parlors. At the door, she commented, "This would be a great place to host the book group."

Ah, the real reason behind her invite surfaced. "I could provide delicious refreshments, too?"

Felicity's hands went together in an understated clap. "That would be grand." The woman slipped out before Donna could tell her what she could do with her invitation. Maybe she shouldn't be so reactive. Have the ladies over, throw out a few appetizers, and get a feel for the good people of the neighborhood. It might help to look at the invitation.

She slid one finger under the flap of the heavy vellum envelope and opened it. Elaborate, cursive lettering announced the book club would meet to discuss a local history book a week from now. She flipped open the invitation to see that the event would be held at The Painted Lady Inn. She'd been hoodwinked by soft-spoken Felicity, who even had her agreeing the inn would be a perfect place for the book club meeting, announcing it as such before she was even asked. The nerve. The envelope caught fire as Donna held it over a lighted scented candle. The heavy stock flared up, forcing her to throw the flaming missive into the empty fireplace. Too bad she couldn't toss the book club into the fireplace, too.

Chapter Two

T HE WARM, YEASTY scent of cinnamon date rolls filled the kitchen as Donna lifted them from the oven. Her cell phone burbled at the same time. Tennyson had carried the chilled juices and water into the dining room but he hadn't come back. Donna's left eye twitched, fearing he might be lecturing someone about the meaninglessness of life. Those on a holiday getaway preferred to think of life as a party, something to enjoy. Too bad J. E. Muscovy didn't have that attitude.

Donna clamped her back molars together as she once again considered the possibility of the critic popping out of her bedroom like an evil jack-in-the-box for breakfast. Maria was off on a mission to buy Irish butter since the grass-fed butter the inn normally bought from a local dairy might not be good enough. Her sister-in-law was also on the lookout for exotic fruits such as dragon fruit and Kakadu plums to add to the fruit compote.

The phone had stopped ringing, but then started up again. It could be Maria telling her how all they had left was European-style butter. She placed the buns on the counter before grabbing the phone.

"Hello."

A whispered voice asked, "Donna?"

"Of course it's Donna. Whom am I speaking to?" Why hadn't she looked at the number before she answered it?

"It's me, Janice."

The breathy voice did sound like her friend. "Why are you whispering?"

"I didn't want her to overhear."

A quick review of Janice's family members didn't include any females. "Who?"

"You know, J. E." Her voice carried a tinge of fear.

"Janice, she's here at my inn, not over there. Trust me, she doesn't have bionic ears."

"Oh yeah, right." A nervous laugh carried over the line. "What's she like?"

"Imagine the wicked stepmother from *Cinderella*, a self-important diva, and a demanding family matriarch all in one body. Also imagine that person dressed in black with her nose so high in the air it's lucky she doesn't trip."

The back door slammed as a windblown Maria dashed into the kitchen brandishing two grocery bags. The woman put down the bags, washed her hands, and pulled out the fruit compote made last night.

"Good. It will make her easy to recognize."

"No doubt. I have to finish breakfast. I have more easily pleased guests waiting to eat."

"Wait!"

Donna had already turned the oven off and pulled out the breadbaskets with her free hand, certain her friend had nothing else to say. Donna clutched the cell phone between her neck and shoulder. "What?"

"Could you spy on her?"

Her hands stopped in the act of lining the bread baskets with floral cloth napkins. "Did I hear you right? This isn't a reality television show. I don't have time to go dogging the woman's steps."

"Oh, nothing like that. Tell me when she leaves and if she's headed my way."

She lifted the flaky pastries into the basket and needed to get them to the guests while still warm. "Fine. Bye."

She put down the phone the same time Tennyson entered the room. "Here, take the rolls out." The slow-moving student blinked when she shoved the breadbaskets at him but then returned to the dining room. Most of her guests assumed Tennyson was her son and often complimented him for helping his mother out. Strange that he never bothered to correct them.

"Who was on the phone?" Maria looked up from peeling the dragon fruit.

Another buzzer chirped, forcing Donna to hold up one finger as she rushed to their second oven to pull out perfectly crisped bacon. It only took her a couple of guests to learn that no matter what tasty morning delicacy she served, there would always be those who insisted on bacon. The toaster oven pinged, signaling the heating time for the soy sausage patties was done. On a good day, the vegetarians and meat eaters didn't share a table.

"Janice." She patted the bacon dry and placed it on a serving platter. Some of the items she served on a plate while others she left on the server with identifying cards for the guests to help them- selves. The bacon's card would read organic whey-fed pork bacon. Most people didn't know what whey was, but it sounded natural so they were good with it. "She wants me to spy on our," Donna lifted her fingers to make quote marks, "special guest."

"Are you going to do it?" Maria spooned the compote into glass sherbet bowls.

Donna allowed herself an eye roll at the idea. "Are you kidding me? I need to get started on the girls' weekend out special."

"Remember," she emphasized the last word, "you thought Janice might pop for a two-for-one coupon. You've got to do something for her to get her to do something for you."

Maria was right. She hated it when that happened. "You have a point."

Tennyson slipped into the kitchen. He flattened himself against a cupboard. "She's up. She'll not be dining with the rabble, but would like a strong Irish coffee, multi-grain toast with Kerrygold butter and orange marmalade, the traditional kind with pepper."

"Good job on remembering." Donna complimented her helper, who hadn't always shown an aptitude for the hospitality industry.

Tennyson's skin had blanched to an even paler shade of white if that were possible. "I had to. She shot me with those laser eyes of hers, and it felt like she was searing the words into my very soul."

Maria flourished a small foil package. "Got the butter. You hit that one on the head. Who ever heard of pepper in marmalade?"

"Better yet, is it ground pepper or pepper flakes, which we can easily insert and put it in a small relish dish?" Donna rushed around the kitchen assembling a small tray while Maria put the bread in the toaster. The red pepper flakes gave the marmalade a bit of a tang. If she used too much, J.E. would accuse her of trying to destroy her palate.

When they finished the tray, she presented it to Tennyson. "Go deliver it."

The young man slid his back down the cabinets until he was sitting on the floor. "Don't make me do it. I'm still relatively young."

Jasper barked as Daniel strode into the kitchen.

"Thought I'd drop in for some coffee and a pastry before I headed out to work."

Both women turned in unison. Donna held out the tray. "I'd be glad to get you a pastry, but you need to deliver this tray first."

Daniel cast a glance at the whimpering Tennyson. "I assume it's the critic."

"You assume right. Besides, I have to cut and plate the frittata. I know you're a big frittata fan." She pushed the tray into her brother's ready hands and turned back to the stove.

Tennyson stood and made ready to exit through the back door.

Donna spoke without turning from the stove. "Stop!"

Tennyson froze with his hand on the doorknob. "You're almost as scary as she is."

The *almost* part bothered her. "If you're determined to stay out of the range of J.E.'s laser eyes, then you can do the laundry. I'll need clean sheets and towels for when we make up the rooms later."

Tennyson sighed, which with him was an acknowledgment he'd heard.

"Follow the directions on the fabric softener crystals this time. Last time, I had to rewash the sheets because they were flowery enough to attract a swarm of bees."

"Okay," he muttered and disappeared into the laundry room sanctuary.

Maria lifted the platter with the fruit compotes on it. Donna followed with the frittatas and small pitchers of homemade salsa. They entered the dining room smiling. Maria asked the guests if they slept well while Donna attempted to pry out their plans for the day so she'd know when to clean their rooms.

The sound of an interior door closing caught her attention. Had the mysterious J.E. come to dine with the riff-raff? It was Daniel. He strode past the dining room with no obvious wounds or missing limbs. Donna hurried to the kitchen anxious to get the lowdown.

But first, she'd have to get the bacon, sausage, and toast out on the sideboard. It would be best to hoard her Irish butter and improvised marmalade for tomorrow. J.E. only booked for two nights, which meant whoever's restaurant she'd savage would happen today.

Normally, Donna stood at the perimeter of the dining room, watching the guests eat. It really was her favorite time of day. Overall, everyone really enjoyed her cooking, except for that one lactose-intolerant man. It would have been helpful if he'd mentioned that when he booked. Today, she'd had to forgo her pleasure to get the lowdown so she could relay it to Janice. Her sudden, impulsive action to send Daniel wasn't inspired. The fact he was dressed in his construction clothes might appeal to some secret fantasy. At least he was clean since he had just started his day.

Daniel nursed a cup of coffee as he sat at the kitchen bar.

"I owe you big time. As you can tell, J.E.'s laser gaze devastated Tennyson. He's doing laundry now." She pulled out the large slice of frittata she'd left warming in the oven. "Salsa?"

"Ketchup." Her brother winked with his entreaty.

Donna retrieved it from the fridge. "Good thing you're not eating out in the dining room. I would have to refuse your request."

"Yeah." He chuckled. "I know better. You would have put the ketchup in a cut glass dish, stirred some herbs into it, and called it gourmet tomato sauce."

He had her there. Brothers knew you too well. "What's our critic up to today?

Daniel upended the ketchup bottle, splattering the frittata with red. "She's going to meet a friend. Asked me where the Little Bit of Paris Café was."

Despite the name, the place was little more than a sandwich shop that served wine. No way the critic came all the way from New

York to review the place. It might be possible she did have a friend, and they were going to meet there. So far, the only beverages the woman asked for were alcoholic. She'd want to meet in a bar. As soon as Daniel left, she'd call Janice.

The front bell jingled, which was a surprise. All the guests were here, unless someone was leaving. Donna stood, ready to go to the side door to see which guest was leaving for the day. At least she'd know what room to clean first.

Maria came in through the swinging door carrying an empty juice pitcher. "Herman's here, and his granddaughter is visiting."

The white-haired neighbor entered, followed by a slender girl with a cascade of shiny dark hair. She looked as if she was barely out of her teens, but sometimes it was hard to tell. Donna had noticed she frequently thought people were younger than they actually were. It was difficult not to call anyone under thirty a kid.

Herman greeted everyone and then gestured to his granddaughter. "This is Winnie. She's visiting with me. Came to videotape my memoirs for some living history project."

Daniel nodded with a full mouth while Maria smiled and patted Herman's shoulders, telling him, "I'm sure you're very proud."

Donna plated up two extra date buns and placed them on the counter. "Coffee?" She knew Herman drank it, but wasn't sure about Winnie.

The girl in question gave her a shy smile and then answered, "Yes, please."

Good manners. You always had to like that in a young person. Donna nipped into the dining room and made a casual survey between tables to make sure everyone had what they wanted. She cleared the dishes from an abandoned table and picked up the tablecloth, carefully holding up the four corners so no crumbs would tumble to the floor. Underneath the tablecloth waited another pristine tablecloth. A trick she'd learned eating at some of the better restaurants. The drawback was if the diner spilled something, then all the tablecloths were history.

The dirty dishes and cloth went behind a screen until the dining room was empty. A few of the guests complimented her breakfast, making her blush with pride. She wondered if the early leavers had enjoyed theirs. Not everyone remarked on her breakfast, just expecting it to be good, the same way they expected the sun to come up. If it didn't meet their particular standards, they'd rant about it on numerous review sites.

Donna placed the coffee cups on a small tray, thinking Winnie and Tennyson might be the same age. Who knew? They could be friends eventually. She rejected the idea as soon as it came. Herman's granddaughter had little in common with the melancholy Tennyson, who could be morose in any situation. When she asked what could be wrong with kittens, he answered with the possibility of catching pink eye from handling them too much.

Donna could hear the voices as she backed into the door. Herman had started on his lost diamonds story again. It must be for Winnie's benefit since all of them had heard it before, also chapters two and three, plus the alternate versions. Herman tended to vary the story in the telling. It was hard to know if he couldn't remember or if he was testing them to see if they were listening.

Daniel, Maria, and Winnie had their heads angled in Herman's direction. Tennyson had his head propped in his hand. Instead of looking at Herman, his gaze was stuck on Winnie. The goofy expression meant he liked what he saw. If she didn't know better, she'd have thought he had spotted the first female ever created. Adam probably had a similarly besotted look when he spotted Eve.

Herman noticed her and grinned. "Well, that's about it. The diamonds were never found."

Winnie's brow furrowed slightly. "Did no one look for them?"

Her grandfather reached for his cup and took a long sip, then swallowed. "Yes, they did. Many people did. It was rather like those treasure ships that went down hundreds of years ago. Everyone thinks they know where it is, but finding it is an entirely different matter."

The diamond story always rattled her, and not because she believed there were jewels hidden on her property. It wouldn't do for others to think something valuable rested under her oak tree or the recently varnished floorboards. Strangers sneaking in to dig up her yard would be bad enough. She didn't need the extra issue of guests thumping the walls trying to find a secret entrance or prying up the floor. Her initial urge was to tell the elderly man to desist with his story. Donna couldn't, though. She realized this was Herman's claim to fame and his entrance into most conversations with an alleged crime committed so long ago most had never heard about it. Maria had suggested they research the topic to find out more about it. If they had and discovered the robbery never happened, it would only embarrass her neighbor.

Before Winnie could get any ideas about resurrecting the research idea, Donna made sure to add her two cents. "Those treasure hunters on the lookout for sunken ships are in open waters. If the diamonds were buried somewhere, they'd be on private property and belong to whoever owned the property." That should settle the matter.

Tennyson chose that moment to shake off his hormone-induced lethargy. "Oh, no, if it's stolen, it goes back to the original owners. Don't you remember the Nazi-stolen art?"

Truthfully, she hadn't kept up on any Nazi art cases.

Daniel chimed in about some case involving art stolen from a museum. The museum didn't get it back since the owner bought it in good faith, not knowing it was stolen. The jingle of the bell attached to the front door had her peeking out the window, unwilling to be part of the legal debate. J.E. Muscovy meandered down the porch steps and took a left toward the parking lot.

Donna blinked, making sure it was the critic. The false eyelashes, plunging neckline, and upward turn of the lips confused her, but the black ensemble and superior tilt of the head confirmed it. The woman would get away before she could follow. At least she had a hint about the woman's destination, unless J.E. had lied to Daniel.

Her hand grasped her apron and tore it off over her head. She sprinted for the back door, grabbing her keys and purse. Jasper, mistaking her flight for a game, ran after her, frantically barking.

Maria called after her. "Where are you going?"

"Fact-finding mission." She didn't say more due to the company gathered in the kitchen, especially Herman. Give the man a tidbit and it would be all over town.

As she grabbed the door to pull it shut, she heard her sister-in-law explain. "She's spying on the food critic to get BOGOF coupons."

When put that way, it made her sound desperate and cheap.

Chapter Three

THE WHITE RENTAL car slowed for a stop sign and then turned right without making a complete stop. Donna sucked in her lips, debating how close she should follow. If she hadn't seen the sedan pull out of the inn's lot, she'd have no clue what the critic drove. Legacy practically sat on the South Carolina borderline. The farther south one the lighter the cars became due to the heat. No one who had lasted an entire summer would ever be foolish enough to buy a black car with a black interior. Unfortunately, this resulted in the majority of the rental cars being white or silver.

A white SUV crossed from the side road. Now there'd be two white cars in front of her. Not good, not good at all. Donna sucked in her lips as she eyed the SUV's broad frame. It made it impossible to know if J.E. had turned anywhere. That's what she got for lagging behind.

Her foot pressed the accelerator, putting her on the SUV's tail, which allowed her to examine the driver's stick people stickers along with a boy in the back seat sticking his tongue out at her. The vehicle's speed dropped. It could be a way to irritate her for tailgating, or the driver could be on the phone, oblivious to what was happening around her. Donna's foot eased up on the gas, putting some space between them. Good thing, too since the SUV turned abruptly into a side street without signaling.

"Geez, Louise, does anyone know how to drive in this town?"

The lack of the automotive behemoth allowed her to see in front of her. A white sedan, about seven car lengths ahead, eased into a traffic circle. The only thing between her and the car were two scooters. The male teens steered brightly colored glorified mopeds while their girlfriends precariously balanced behind them. It explained why the previous vehicle had slowed and turned. Instead of appreciating young love, Donna wondered why they couldn't follow traffic rules and ride single file. It would have been relatively easy to pass one of them, but two would be chancier.

A large semi rumbled by, leaving a breeze in its wake and causing the young lovers to weave toward the shoulder. She swerved to the left, anxious to get past them, but she misjudged the speed of the sedan approaching from the other way. The car flew past her with the horn blaring as its wheels cut into the shoulder. There were only a few inches between them. Certainly close enough to see the red-faced, middle-aged man driving who unfortunately looked very familiar. Ah, maybe he didn't recognize her. She moderated her speed with the plan to blend in with the other drivers. A whine of a siren and a flash of light meant he intended to play hardball. *Great.*

The scooter teens had the temerity to point as they whizzed by. Mark Taber had just made a U-turn and was stopping her and not those rule breakers. Her target was getting away. Maybe the woman *was* heading to the café. Mark parked his car behind her and approached on the left. A button push lowered her driver window.

"Donna, would you care to tell me what you are doing?"

Even though Mark looked perturbed as he squatted to peer into her window, he wasn't that mad. He'd had the same expression when Jasper peed on his shoes. No harm had come to her dog then.

It might not be wise to mention she was tailing a critic for Janice. The silence lengthened as she thought of a reasonable excuse. "I needed to get around the scooters. Did you notice they were riding side by side?"

Mark cleared his throat, shook his head, then coughed, delaying whatever he intended to say. "It was hard to see anything when almost being run off the road. My attention was on not hitting you or rolling my car. Due to my years of driving expertise, I managed to do both."

A disbelieving snort erupted before Donna could rethink the advisability of such a response. "Please, it wasn't that bad. No one was hurt. Can I go now?" Who knew what J.E. could be up to?

"Tell me why I shouldn't give you a ticket, Donna Tollhouse?" The question sounded more like an ultimatum in his gravelly timbre.

What did women do to get out of tickets? Every female had some go-to trick from crying to flirting. Donna had never ever been pulled over until now. Tears might be hard to pretend since she'd never been a crier. Then again, that would make them more effective. She glanced at the detective who had that befuddled look men often assumed around women. An idea!

Donna leaned forward as much as the seat belt would allow and kissed Mark on the nose. "You're so cute when you go all official."

Mark blushed, grinned, and withdrew his head from the car window opening. "That works. See you later. Drive safe."

The car threw gravel as she accelerated onto the road faster than she intended. A quick glance in the rearview mirror revealed Mark shaking his finger at her. Well, at least he wasn't following her, sirens blaring. A Little Bit of Paris was a small bistro with tables out on the sidewalk. For reasons Donna never quite understood, tourists enjoyed eating outside almost on the road with the sound of traffic and noxious fumes. Even though she'd never visited the café, she thought she knew where it was. Before it became a bistro, it had been The Pancake Hut, before that, The Taco Shack.

Traffic picked up the closer she got to the center of town. A car idling in front of her, waiting for someone to pull out, reminded her that parking spaces came at a premium. The next open spot she should grab no matter how many blocks she had to walk; it might be the only one for a mile. Obviously, the other drivers shared similar thoughts since the traffic crawled. It gave Donna a chance to play her mental game of *tourist, not a tourist*. The women dressed in heels, dark suits, and carrying briefcases, not tourists. The family wearing matching tie-dyed T-shirts, tourists. Too easy. Before she could contemplate why a family would want to wear similar shirts, a jeep backed out, forcing her to inch back to accommodate it. How handy! She'd just zoom into the place. As she inched back a little more, she flicked on her blinker to notify everyone behind her of her intentions. No reason to get anyone else's hopes up.

The jeep cleared the space, straightened, and preceded on its way. Donna put her car in drive, but before she could tap the gas a large Cadillac bumped into the former empty place. Its front bumper even nicked the curb with a metallic scrape. *Really?* Her closed fist slammed the horn. Her small car's horn had all the ferocity of a toy dog barking. Two white-haired ladies popped out of the car. One had a cane, which made Donna regret her honking until the woman flipped her off. Her hand hit the horn again more out of shock than intention. Old ladies had taken a walk on the thug side.

It took three more circles before she found a place in front of the adult toys and lingerie store. Yeah, of course, it would be the only open place. Since the place opened a year ago, it did a brisk business, but locals attributed that to the out-of-towners. People tried not to park in front of the store even if they were customers. If a friend mentioned seeing her car, she'd immediately say her destination was somewhere else. That's exactly what everyone else said.

By this time, J.E. may have met her friend and moved on to a different locale. Donna lunged out of the car, locking it with her fob. Thankful for her long legs, she strode past the storefront windows outlined in purple lights. A quick sideways glance at the display confused more than it revealed. What was the mannequin wearing? Better yet, how did you get something like that on or off?

A young mother pushed a stroller and herded two more children in front of her. "Keep going. It's not nice to stare."

Were the words mainly directed at the children or her since she'd stopped in the middle of the sidewalk? Probably both. A burst of speed left mama and her chicks far behind. The continual existence of the clock shop on the corner puzzled her, but she'd not make the mistake of stopping and staring at it. Her head swivels resembled one of those old-fashioned wind-up toys. J.E. may have finished her meet-up and could be sharing the sidewalks with the hundred other people out today by now.

Normally, all the visitors would excite her because it meant revenue for the town and potential business for her. Today, she found herself in a human obstacle course. A bicycle messenger had her jumping to the right. An amorphous mass of teenagers staring at their phones had her stepping off the curb to avoid them since the likelihood of them looking up was nil.

In the distance, she could see the plywood cutout of the Eiffel Tower that marked the café. Never had she welcomed the sight of a tacky affectation more. Her steps slowed as she wondered how she should play this. Unlike most of the diners, she didn't stop by for a pastry and coffee since she had better at the inn. Why would she even be here?

A woman sitting at an outdoor table waved at her. She looked somewhat familiar, although that far away Donna couldn't place her. Her eyes lit up as a figurative light bulb glowed over her head. She had just stopped by the café to meet a friend. Yes! That would work. Too bad she had no clue what the woman's name was. Smiling, she strolled up to the woman.

"Good morning. What are you up to this fine morning?" Inwardly, she cringed thinking how much she resembled a coffee commercial.

"Donna! Am I glad to see you."

The woman knew her name, which gave her the advantage. Donna's eyes wandered around the unoccupied wrought iron tables littered with empty coffee cups and saucers. No sign of J.E., which meant she'd not come here, she'd already left, or was inside. More likely, she was inside, trying her best not to be recognized.

"Really, why is that?" If they had been good friends, at least she should remember her name. The burgundy dress, the coiffed hair, the ageless face—thanks to plastic surgery—meant she must be a neighbor.

The woman reached up to tap Donna's arm with her long burgundy talons while emitting a forced giggle. "You're having the book group at your inn. I'm in charge of refreshments, which is why I'm here." Her nose crinkled as she gestured to her surroundings.

The woman acted as if she was sitting in a cat box. Somehow, she had missed the appeal of the cute table and a wide-mouth cup of aromatic coffee with a touch of nutmeg. Her hand cupped beside her face, as if she intended to whisper, she instead spoke in an overloud voice. "The food here is awful."

Ah, yes, now she remembered. *Bernice*, the loud whisperer.

She'd announced at the Inn's open house that Daniel could put his boots under her bed anytime, which earned her a look of impending death from Maria. Before she could ask why she was here, the woman went on to explain.

"My job is to find the right treats for our meetings. Our events are more adventurous than this pedestrian fare. I need something that hits the right note. You know what I mean. Your radish anchovy canapes were divine. Everyone raved about your pomegranate guacamole. The blondies were to die for."

This felt like a set-up. If so, the book club members were better sleuths than she was. How did they know where she was heading when she didn't know five seconds before she left? Could it all be serendipitous? It would all depend on if Bernice asked her to provide refreshments for the meeting at her inn.

A male server in a striped shirt and beret came out and asked if she wanted anything. Donna demurred, but Bernice didn't.

"Loren, could you wrap up the napoleons and four eclairs for me?"

"*Oui*, madame." He nodded and hot footed it back into the restaurant.

Donna bet he didn't want to be seen with the eye pencil mustache on his upper lip or the beret. Hadn't Bernice called him by name and ordered food without looking at the menu, proving she was a frequent patron? "Sounds like you're bringing home some yummies."

"Oh, these aren't for me. They're for the children. They have such unrefined palates."

She had no answer to that since she couldn't even remember if the woman had children. What she needed to do was talk to Loren or at least get inside the restaurant. She waved at Bernice. "Good seeing you." She pretended not to hear the loud whispered "wait" for what she was sure would be some artless request for her to make all the goodies she had made previously for the open house. No, thank you. She might not be able to figure out J.E. Muscovy's antics, but it wasn't too hard to read the book club's.

The dim restaurant interior made it hard to make out much, especially when she'd just left the sunlit exterior. There were more bistro tables, a few booths along the wall, and a bar against the back, close to the restrooms. Only a few patrons remained at the bar, while a lone server cleared the dirty tables. No sign of J.E. or her friend, there was no one here if she discounted the men near the bar. Although, it was a social club. A lingering law on the state books made any place that served alcohol obligated to serve food, too. It also merited the less judgmental term, *social club*. Thank goodness the inn didn't fall under that particular law.

She ducked into the bathroom, giving Loren time to deliver the bill and pastries. Black-and-white posters of Paris crowded the small room. The owner wasn't a believer in less-is-more style. After a full ten minutes, she decided the slowest of the slow could have paid the bill and left by now.

When she exited, everyone was gone, including the two patrons, the bartender, and Loren. A tired looking blonde stood at the counter refilling salt shakers.

Donna approached the woman with a smile noting her nametag. Her father had given her a book when she was twelve on how to make friends. Obviously, her parent thought she wasn't good at it. The only useful information she got from it was everyone liked to hear his or her name. "Where is everyone, Danae?"

"Loren and Dirk are out back smoking."

That didn't sound like any place she wanted to be. One employee should be as good as the next. "I was supposed to meet a friend here. A woman with dark hair." She held her hand up to her chin. "Cut about this short. She usually wears black. Did you see anyone like that?"

The server's brow furrowed as she mulled over the question. "Hard to say. Several visitors wore black, and some of them were women. Around nine, we have a glut of people. The rush lasts until about now. No one really sticks out except for that yummy Chef Sylvestor."

Donna couldn't help but notice that the woman's face beamed at the mention of the womanizing restaurateur. Obviously, he had yet another female fan. She couldn't understand the man's magnetism.

The employee shook a shaker packing down the salt before she poured more in. She glanced up briefly and asked, "Was there anything special about your friend that you're looking for?"

Acting superior and being demanding might qualify as special. Then again, maybe half the tourists copped a similar attitude. Donna shrugged. The woman didn't seem to have come here. Perhaps her real destination was so secret she didn't want anyone to know. The conversation she overheard stuck in her mind.

Was she here to evaluate an old friend's restaurant? If so, that should take the pressure off Janice since they weren't friends. Danae called out after her. "Hope you find your friend."

She almost corrected her, saying she wasn't looking for her friend, but that would contradict her earlier statement. Her undercover work could use a little tweaking here and there. The crowds on the sidewalk had dissipated, allowing her to stroll to her car unobstructed. It gave her time to admire the unique shops that had popped up all over the square, everything from a make your own pottery studio to a nail salon that specialized in watercolor manicures. Her steps slowed as she considered the dead end.

The mad dash to the town square, replaying in her mind, stopped at the shocked expression on Mark's face when she'd kissed him. A giggle slipped out. Donna surveyed the people walking toward her two blocks away and likely to turn before they reached her. Another chuckle slipped out, then another. Before she knew it, she was alternatively gasping for air and wiping her eyes. The older couple she'd noticed before hadn't turned and instead made a wide berth around her when they passed.

The woman loudly commented to her companion. "Shameful. Drunk, and it's not even noon."

Her normal abrupt response system kicked into action and she straightened her spine, sending her sense of outrage into a ther-mometer-busting high. All she had to do was march up to the woman and explain that her giddiness came from kissing a cop to get out of a ticket. Yeah, that would convince her she was a solid citizen. The thought caused another laughing fit. She wove a bit as she walked to her car, giving credibility to the woman's claim.

As for Janice, she wouldn't call her yet. Maybe she could discover something useful while cleaning J.E.'s room. The critic probably didn't leave a handy to-do list with items such as get pedicure and skewer someone's career. Without her at the inn to whip Tennyson into action, he was probably lost in a daydream featuring Herman's granddaughter, Winnie. Maria had to get to her accounting job which left no one to pick up the towels and strip the beds. Tennyson would help only if given directives. It also helped to get things done if he had an afternoon class since he buzzed through the work to get to class on time. He hadn't quite grasped that guests didn't enjoy the inconvenience of being deprived of their room while it was cleaned.

A waiting car almost clipped her fender, the driver obviously anxious to get into the available space. "This town needs a parking garage." That would ruin the small-town atmosphere the Chamber of Commerce liked to promote. One brochure even listed it as the inspiration behind a popular vintage television program. It wasn't, though.

Traffic thinned out as she moved away from the town center. The empty country road tempted. Her foot pressed down on the pedal, giving her compact a boost of gas. The four-cylinder engine usually had a time-lapse reaction, resulting in the car jerking before it went faster. The empty strip mall with the abandoned combination bike repair and quickie mart flashed by on her left. A sedan sat in the shadow of the building.

Oh no, another cop. She slowed, waiting for the inevitable. Her phone rang. What now?

"Hello?" Her response sounded terse in her own ears. Why shouldn't it, when she knew a ticket she couldn't afford was in her future, even though the rearview mirror didn't show any flickering lights.

"Donna."

It was Mark Taber, which meant the car lurking in the shadows might have been him. Didn't the town have any crimes for him to solve?

She managed to mellow out her tone. "Hi, Mark. What's happening?"

"Besides you working on another traffic violation? I never realized what a kamikaze driver you were."

"Ha ha. Kamikaze pilots were suicidal. I'm just a little late."

The man had a sense of humor, one of the many things she liked about him. He also hadn't come after her, another plus.

"I'd like you to arrive alive. Besides, even as cute as you are, you can't always kiss your way out of trouble."

Ah, he had called her *cute*. Too bad she was already too far away to wave at him. A smile stretched ear to ear as she held the phone up to her ear. "Aw, I bet you expect a home cooked meal for that remark."

"Wouldn't turn one down. I think you know that." His amusement carried over the phone. "Between your nursing job and the inn, you're a hard woman to catch."

The man had summed up her life in one sentence. It's no wonder she had no social life. "The only time I see you is if there has been a murder in the vicinity."

A heavy sigh carried over the line. "I'd like to change that. Surely Legacy is crime-free for a while. That's why I have traffic detail. As far as I can tell, the only issue with that is a certain innkeeper who's managing to keep me busy."

"It's not like I'm trying. Janice asked me to…" She managed to stop herself before she confessed all. Even though her amateur sleuth skills were somewhat helpful in previous cases, Mark never entirely saw it that way. The man worried too much about her getting hurt or contaminating the crime scene.

"Janice asked you to do what?"

"Oh, nothing really." She hoped to deflect his interest with a non-answer. Although she'd have just as much luck dragging home a bag of salmon and not be followed by a slew of cats.

"Come on, I know you better than that. What had you lead footing it through town?"

How did the man do it? She wiggled her hips as she kept a sedated foot on the gas. No wonder he had no trouble getting confessions. Mark made it feel conversational, not confrontational. Her intention was not to mention it because he'd point out she was violating some type of public ordinance. Then he'd hit her with *Ignorance of the law is not an excuse.*

"Janice wanted to know if the food critic staying at the inn was going to review The Croaking Frog."

"That seems reasonable. Did you ask her?"

Was the man for real? "No, I didn't ask her. These things are top secret. Sometimes the critics even disguise themselves when visiting a restaurant."

"How much of a disguise would the critic need? There's only two types of people in Legacy, local and not local."

He did have that part right. "She might be afraid someone might have seen her photo and recognize her."

"Is she hideous?"

"No." Her behavior could use some adjustment, but the rest of her was average.

"Gorgeous?"

"No."

"Then no one would look twice at her."

Was that the cop talking or the man? Donna decided not to ask. Some things she didn't want to know. "It would matter to you if you were a chef and you knew she was in town. Every person who walked through the restaurant door would get a thorough once-over."

"I guess all the chefs will have to be on their toes, then."

"Yeah, I guess you're right. I wouldn't want to be a chef right now."

"Aren't you?"

"Let's not talk about it." The secret to a good relationship is knowing when not to state the obvious. Her street sign with its ornate edges and curlicues appeared on her left. "I'm almost home."

"Great. Remember, no funny stuff."

It was better not to question the nature of funny stuff. "See you soon. I have a pot roast with your name on it. There's some Idaho spuds just waiting to be transformed into garlic mashed potatoes."

Mark's moan carried across the airwaves. "Cheesecake, too?"

"It could happen." She guided the car into the almost deserted parking lot, which meant most of the guests were gone, perfect for room cleaning. "Home now. Gotta go."

She hung up the phone while the man was still panting after her cheesecake. Her mother may not have taught her much about men, but she had mentioned always leave them wanting more. At the time, her momma might not have been talking about pot roast.

Chapter Four

THE ONLY ONE to welcome Donna home was Jasper. His grand greeting consisted of barking and running to his empty food bowl. Someone forgot to feed her pup. Okay, that someone was her, but seriously, did she have to do everything around here?

Maria and Daniel were both gone to their respective jobs, leaving an eerie stillness. The last time the house had been this quiet, she had found a stiff in her upstairs parlor. She crept around her own inn as if she were trespassing. Finally, she found Tennyson on the third floor, explaining to Winnie in lurid detail about the body Donna'd found. This was not the story she wanted to be associated with the B and B. "Tennyson, don't you have rooms to clean?"

He turned bewildered eyes on her as if he'd never seen her in his life. He gave himself a little shake, then smiled at Winnie over his shoulder and addressed his comment to her. "Ah, the work of an innkeeper is never done."

Winnie nodded. "No problem. Maybe I'll see you around."

The girl headed for the stairs. Tennyson trailed after her. "I'd like that. Maybe we could see a movie or get a pizza. The bay is beautiful on a moonlit night." His voice grew fainter as he accompanied Winnie down the steps.

Donna wanted to explain to him how the "maybe I'll see you around" was a throwaway line that meant nothing. It was up there with "Let's do lunch sometime." If a person truly wanted to see you, he or she made plans. No use talking to Tennyson, though. He wouldn't believe her.

Normally, she did half the rooms and then rechecked the rooms Tennyson did. As a man, he didn't always understand why a woman might freak out if she spotted a hair strand that didn't match her own. Dust didn't offend him either, but he did process the fact that his boss wanted the dust gone.

Returning to the first floor, Donna armed herself with clean towels and sheets and made her way to the critic's room. After J.E.'s various demands, she expected the room to be trashed. The tray with her morning dishes sat on the small drum table. The bedspread had been pulled up in a halfhearted attempt to make the bed. The suitcase remained zipped. In the bathroom, a toiletry bag hung from the shower rod. As far as she could see, there was no evidence anywhere. She guessed it all depended on what she was looking for.

Sometimes, it amazed her that people could stay at her inn and leave nothing of themselves behind. Then there were the guests who left clothes, eyeglasses, even dentures she had to mail back to the owners. Donna hummed a little as she stripped the bed, thinking of Mark's face. She stretched the high thread count sheets across the mattress, speculating if the critic even observed the quality. People noticed when something wasn't there, rather like cleanliness. She smoothed her hand over the sheet, pushing out any wrinkles.

Donna ran a shammy over the furniture, picking up any dust that had dared to fall within the last twenty-four hours. The HEPA filter on her heating and air system not only cut down on mold and mildew, but also caught dust and dog hair, which prevented complaints about Jasper.

The dust mop skimming over the wood floor served as her final touch before vacuuming the area rug. Her knees had the nerve to whisper a protest by cracking as she bent to mop under the bed. It was the weather, not her age, that caused her knees to pop.

A bright orange sticky note stuck to the mop head. Donna plucked it off and held her arm out to read *Sylvester, Norelle, The Croaking Frog, Culinary Cousins* written in bold script. The last one she hadn't heard of, which meant it wasn't in Legacy. Sylvester's had a bold line struck through it. Did the line mean J.E. decided not to review it or had she already? Were the other restaurants on the list to be reviewed? If so, J.E. expected to get quite a bit done during her short stay. Too bad the woman couldn't be more explicit in notes to herself.

Donna placed the note on the bedside table, unwilling to toss it back under the bed, which would imply she hadn't cleaned there. At least she could credit J.E with being reasonably neat. It only took her a few minutes to clean the bathroom.

On the second floor, she found Tennyson staring out the window in the direction of Herman's house. "Tennyson, do you have classes today?"

He jerked before swinging around. "What day is it?"

"It's Friday." Love, or at least infatuation, could do a number on the average male.

His hand rubbed his chin, reminding her of Mark as he worked through an issue. A panicked look replaced the contemplative one as Tennyson patted down his body before pulling his cell phone out of a pocket. He powered it on and twitched. "It's ten o'clock. I have New World Philosophy at ten-thirty. If I'm late, Dr. DeGeneres will view it as a personal statement."

He dashed past her and took the stairs two at a time. Donna peered out the window, keeping an eye on his running form as he climbed into his dated car and tore out of the parking lot. A sigh escaped her. Tennyson's abrupt departure would result in a visit from the neighborhood council, who'd decided the inn represented a decline in property values. Love could be painful for those around the besotted one, not to mention more work for her since Tennyson hadn't started on a single room.

Her cell rang. It was Janice, which settled her internal debate.

"Hello, Janice."

"What did you find out?"

"Besides every rental agency uses white or silver cars?"

"Everyone knows that."

"J.E. Muscovy moves faster than I do."

An indrawn breath signaled Janice's dismay across the phone lines. "You lost her."

"You're making the assumption that I ever had her. The woman came down the stairs and she was gone. She had mentioned to Daniel going to A Bit of Paris Café."

A snort sounded loud in her ear, summing up Janice's feelings about the place.

"She could have gone there to meet someone as opposed to reviewing the place. Besides, one of the employees admitted to seeing a woman dressed in black." Donna didn't bother to add that she'd seen several people dressed in black. It would only make her appear to be a washout when tailing people.

"That's good. Too bad we don't know who she was going to meet. It could be important."

It probably wasn't as important as Janice assumed. "It could have been a sorority sister. I did find a list in her room." Donna related the names and that Sylvester's had a dark line through it. She expected her friend to be alarmed that her restaurant was on the list.

"Culinary Cousins! Seriously. That place has only been open a year, and they always have these two blond former cheerleaders in all the ads who are supposedly the cousins behind it."

This was news to her. "Where is it?"

Janice continued in a full rant as if she hadn't heard her question. "I doubt if either one of them can cook. It's all supposed to be southern cooking with plenty of butter and fried food."

Sometimes friends knew when to pull the plug. "I have the entire second floor to clean. Talk to you later." Her thumb depressed the end button, but it probably did little to stop Janice's outrage. It made Donna want to try out the restaurant that caused her friend to go all ruffled feathers.

Giggles greeted her when she reached the first room. A *Do Not Disturb* sign indicated she could pass on cleaning it. One down, and three to go. She met one couple leaving who only wanted fresh towels. So far, she was batting a thousand. The third unit was not being used and stood empty. If she had sent Tennyson up to do the work, he'd have reported back that he'd finished without mentioning there wasn't too much to do. After replacing the towels in the second unit and spending about 20 minutes organizing and refilling the snack pantries, Donna clomped down the stairs ready for a coffee break and a possible treat.

Mark Taber's voice drifted from the kitchen. Who was he talking to since Daniel and Maria were gone? She knew the man well enough to know he didn't carry on conversations with himself, at least not both sides. She could also hear another voice.

"Why would someone kidnap a dog?"

Tennyson was back in time to *not* help with the cleaning. Donna pushed the kitchen door open. Mark grinned at her. The half-full coffee pot behind him also brightened her mood. If Tennyson started it, she'd have to forgive him for his witless day so far.

"No class?"

Tennyson glanced up from his seated position at the kitchen island. "No. There was a note on the door. They should have texted." He gestured for Mark to continue.

Donna poured herself a cup of coffee and pulled shortbread cookies out of the bread box.

"That's where she hid them," Tennyson whispered—over-loud.

"Go ahead with the story." She placed the plate in the middle of the island. Both men reached for the shortbread and stuffed their mouths. Donna watched them with an indulgent eye. It was hard to be critical when people liked your food.

"Ah, yes, this is heaven in my mouth." Mark reached for another cookie the same time Tennyson did. The two of them would clean the plate before she even had one. Donna grabbed a cookie, not totally certain neither one of them would growl at her.

"Dog story?" She prompted as she dunked her cookie into her coffee.

"Ah yes, that. There were some lively antics in the Sunblest Neighborhood, so much so that the neighbors called the police to intervene. A couple was going through a divorce."

"That's not surprising."

Mark held up a hand. "Wait until you hear more. Like most divorces, there were things in dispute. Apparently, there was a dog involved."

"They both wanted the dog?"

Tennyson laughed, spewing cookie crumbs. "Wait until you hear more."

Mark cleared his throat, regaining their attention. "The dog in question was an elderly basset hound with a flatulence issue."

"I supposed they both loved the dog very much."

"They could have. They didn't want to drop Loralee at the pound, but neither one wanted the dog. Instead of keeping the dog, they both kept trying to leave the hound at each other's place, usually in the middle of the night. It would have worked if the hound hadn't felt an urge to bay at midnight."

"So what happened?"

Mark rested his head into his upturned palms for a second, never a good sign. There wasn't too much that could overwhelm him. A fight over a dog shouldn't do it.

"The couple was out on the lawn, screaming at each other when the police arrived. When they discovered a dog was involved, they called me. Now that they're divorced, neither one wants the dog. Their aging friend is an impairment to their new lifestyles."

Mark's kindness to four-legged friends was known throughout the city. He often took 911 calls from children whose parents declared there was no hope for a pet hit by a fast-moving delivery truck. He even paid vet bills out of his own pocket. As much as he loved dogs, he never bothered to have any of his own, since he was never home to care for them.

"What did you do…" she paused, trying to remember the dog's name, "…with Loralee?"

Mark's eyes softened, making him even more appealing. He held out his open hands. "I had to take her. I couldn't leave the elderly dog with enraged individuals who kept trying to dump her on each other. All that anger couldn't be good for her. It was no wonder she howled. Loralee needs a peaceful, comfortable place to spend her golden years."

The man had a way with painting an emotional scenario. "You should be doing those voiceovers for dog shelter commercials. Where did you leave her?"

Mark reached across the island for her hand. His fingers wrapped around hers and tightened. The unexpected action caused her to look down at their joined hands. Maybe she did jump start the man's romantic intentions by kissing him today.

Tennyson stood. "I think I'll leave the two of you alone. So you can…" He left the room before even finishing his statement.

Jasper's nails clicked as he moved around the kitchen in search of a dropped tidbit. She did her best to ignore her dog while engaged in a tender moment. There had been so few in her life she wanted to enjoy it. Mark's brown eyes reflected back his sincerity and the tiniest bit of amusement that made no sense. Jasper finished his survey near the back door before erupting into a barking frenzy. A long bay on the other side of the door responded.

"Mark!" She jerked her hand from his. She backed away from the island, keeping her eyes on the man. A quick peek outside revealed a long basset hound with a white muzzle. She lifted her head and gave Donna a long, pleading gaze.

"Okay. I want you to know neither one of you is playing fair."

Jasper took advantage of the door being cracked open and pushed outside. He greeted Loralee with a nose touch, then backed away. The leash tied to the porch railing limited the dog's movements. If Mark had planned on making the dog look pathetic, he couldn't have done a better job.

"Let's get the poor pooch some water." Donna untied the leash and led the dog into the kitchen. Jasper darted ahead, showing more energy than she'd seen in her pup in a long time.

Mark pulled an older plastic bowl from the cabinet and filled it with water. He placed the bowl on the floor and addressed the dog. "Here you go, Loralee. I told you I'd find you a nice place. See, I didn't lie. Donna has a heart of gold."

She snorted at how thick he was laying it on. "Mark, I can't keep the dog, especially with J.E. at the inn. The woman would write an entire column about the reasons dogs ruin B and Bs. She may have already drafted it."

"Where is your poison pen critic now?" he asked from his kneeling position by the dog.

The story about her failed attempt to follow J.E. would not amuse. It would probably earn her another lecture on the dangers of trying to emulate police dramas. She poured some of Jasper's kibble into another plastic bowl. "I imagine she's out murdering someone's culinary career."

"Doesn't the woman like any restaurant?"

While she had become an avid reader of J.E.'s no-holds-barred reviews, it was hard to remember her praising one particular restaurant. "She often compliments one thing, then rips into something else in the next sentence. It is hard to say if she truly likes a restaurant. Take Norelle's for example. She could rave about their shrimp and grits, then bash the place for tacky interior and slow service. I guess it's all what a foodie is looking for. It's easy to overlook a too-chatty hostess or a dark interior. It's hard to forgive bad food."

"Depends." Mark chuckled, then added, "On how hungry you are."

She lifted one eyebrow.

"Your meals are always wonderful."

She remained silent. The only thing she ever learned from doing her surgery round was to remain silent. Even the unconscious patient absorbed all the sounds around them, knitting it into a type of reality. It often served as the slender thread that held the patient on the right side of the ground. The chief surgeon often used silence as a response to stupid inquiries or those he didn't want to answer. Most residents ended up babbling apologies for even asking, whereas Donna stayed observant, refusing to verbalize her inquiries.

Mark babbled, not unlike the residents. "Everything about them is great from the appetizers to the desserts."

"Un-huh. So have you contacted the basset rescue society?"

Mark exhaled loudly, probably glad for the subject change. "I haven't yet, but I will." He fondled Loralee's ears. "She's a good dog. An older person without kids would be the perfect fit for her. Someplace quiet."

"That's not here. You've witnessed how crazy the place can be, especially when we have three or four people in the kitchen trying to get breakfast ready."

Mark's slightly open mouth made him look almost as woebegone as the dog. It was obvious he hadn't thought the matter out. "Why don't you take the dog home? You fit the description of an ideal owner," Donna suggested.

He held up his hands as if she'd pulled a gun on him, instead of asking a legitimate question. "Can't do it. You know I'm never home."

True. He worked overtime, but he probably volunteered for it to give the family men time off. "I imagine a dog like Loralee wouldn't need as much time as a pup. You're in control of your schedule and could run by when needed. In absolute worst cases, I could step in to take care of her. Besides, it would give you a reason to go home. If you have someone waiting for you, you'd want to be home more."

The man opened his mouth, closed it, and finally shook his head. "I wouldn't mind having a special someone waiting for my return. I guess I never expected it would be a dog."

"Dogs are the best." Donna stopped when the meaning behind

Mark's words penetrated. She swallowed once, wanting to make sure she knew what he meant. "You were hoping for a…" Some things were easier in her mental rehearsals than in reality. "…ferret?"

"Yeah, you got it. Every man needs a ferret." His phone chimed, ending what more he might have said.

Donna scooted closer where she could hear better. Mark lifted one eyebrow and thumbed the speaker when she almost leaned against his shoulder.

"An abandoned rental car? Where at?" Mark queried. A voice on his cell phone continued.

"It's on Pearl Road leading out of town right at the patch of woods before you get to the cut-off for the hospital. The citizen who reported it said the engine was running. It wasn't when I arrived, but the fuel gauge registers empty."

"Strange. Not like someone to wander off and leave the car running."

Donna mouthed the words. "Whose car is it?"

Mark took the hint, although he probably would have asked on his own. "Is there any identifying information?" His eyes cut to Donna, possibly in irritation, but she hadn't deciphered his entire range of expressions yet.

"A purse was in the car. The license is for a Jane Ellen Muscovy."

"Okay. Don't touch anything. See you in ten." Mark stood and pocketed his phone. "You heard everything?"

"Yes."

"Can you tell me anything about your guest's movements?"

She knew this was the part where she'd have to confess all. "Daniel told me she'd be at A Little Bit Of Paris. Janice asked me to follow her."

"Why?" Mark had pulled his narrow notebook out of his suit

jacket and held a pen over it.

Donna shrugged. Anything she said would somehow end up sounding goofy. "She thought I could find out if J.E was going to review her place."

"I would have suspected Janice would know, since she operates gossip central."

"Well, she didn't. I tried to follow J.E., but a certain law enforcement lawyer slowed me down. All I found out at the café was a woman possibly answering her description had been there. It wasn't too much to go on since her description consisted of a non-local female dressed in black."

"I could see how that left things wide open. Did you go anywhere else?"

Donna rocked back on her heels and stood. "I couldn't see any reason to try to track her down, especially when I had rooms to clean. I came back here."

"It might be more accurate to say you sped back here."

The man thought he was being humorous.

A metallic thunk of a car door slamming and running feet on the porch stairs had both Mark and Donna staring at the back door as a red-faced woman burst through it.

"J. E.'s portrait is up on Norelle's wall of death!"

Chapter Five

"DIDN'T YOU HEAR me? J.E.'s portrait is on the Wall of Death. You know what that means?" The agitated hand gestures brought Donna's attention to the white butcher apron, liberally spattered with red.

"Janice, what were you doing before you decided to speed over here? Looks to me like you were at the slaughterhouse."

Mark circled the woman. His gaze started at her out-of-control red curls and continued down to her bare feet. "I'd be curious to know that, too, and why you're barefoot."

"Argh." Janice shot both hands through her windblown hair. "What's wrong with you two? If J.E. is on the Wall of Death, she'll never have a chance to taste my award-winning gazpacho."

Her friend's behavior confused her. Donna flapped her hands in front of Janice. "Wait a minute. You didn't want the reviewer to show up at your restaurant. You told me."

"Ah, yeah, I did." Janice walked to the coffee pot and poured herself a cup. "I gotta sit down." She took a seat on a nearby stool. Donna joined her on a matching stool.

"You did want her to come by?" Why had she trailed the woman then if Janice wanted her to come by?

Her friend rubbed the back of her neck as she explained. "You know how vicious J.E.'s reviews can be. She can close a restaurant with her snarky reviews, but people actually get excited when she mentions something good. She could hate everything else about the restaurant, but say they had great coffee or divine cheesecake. Suddenly everyone is showing up for the coffee. It gives people a chance to discover everything isn't horrible. I was hoping my gazpacho would be that one thing."

Did Donna have that one great culinary concoction that would bring people from all over the world to the inn? Most of her desserts were extraordinary, but most places did dessert well, even if they bought them frozen and thawed before serving. "How would you have made her order the gazpacho?"

"Ah," Janice held up one finger. "That was a stroke of brilliance. I made up new menus with an award-winning ribbon over the gazpacho description. It would be like waving a red cape in front of the woman."

The detective leaned against the island. "That could work, but…"

Donna cut him off before he could finish. "I could have killed myself trying to keep up with your critic! The woman has a lead foot. Why didn't you tell me you wanted her to visit? I could have suggested your place."

"You make it sound simple, but—" Janice grimaced. "Call it a calculated risk. Business has been good after the Food Channel spotlight. I even considered expanding. I needed a little something to improve my brand. The Legacy folks visit my restaurant because they know me and my food. The tourists sometimes showed before the Food Channel mention, but mainly they wander in because I'm the only eatery close to…" She wiggled her index and middle fingers in an air quote. "…where Columbus landed." She ended the quote.

Mark cleared his throat, indicating he had something to say, but Janice was unaware of his personal habits and kept talking.

"I needed that extra zing before I consider another restaurant in a different location." Janice cupped her chin in her hand and stared at her coffee.

It had to be hard to see all that possibly slip away. J.E. struck her as someone who never gave false praise or any praise for that matter. Her superiority probably came from her wide experience of 5-star restaurants. It must be hard to tolerate the rather pedestrian efforts of an average chef, and her reviews reflected this attitude. "You know it could have gone the other way. Your restaurant could have been ridiculed."

"Ah, but the gazpacho was my secret weapon. I had confidence it would win her over. I even read where it was one of her favorite dishes."

A light bulb moment happened for Donna as she considered her friend's motives. "You created your tasty soup specifically for J.E."

"I did." Janice sniffed, then used a bent knuckle to wipe away a tear. "A lot of good it did me."

Mark clapped his hands together. "As interesting as this is, I need a few facts before I leave. Did you cause J.E. to come here?"

If so, maybe Donna could take a few lessons and get a top bed and breakfast reviewer to visit The Painted Lady. Too bad Donna couldn't think of any reviewers at the moment.

Janice took a sip of coffee, but held onto the cup. "I mentioned it at a Chamber of Commerce meeting." She cut her eyes to Donna. "Those things you never attend."

"Remember, I still have a day job at the hospital. I'm not free to come and go as I please like you are."

"Ladies, please." Mark's phone chimed again. "They're wondering where I am." He pointed to Janice. "Make it short."

"All of us got the name of a local paper that prints her reviews.

We started an email campaign enlisting other businesses, relatives, and social media friends to ask J.F. to investigate Legacy. It wasn't just me. Every eatery tooted their own horn. I'm not sure how Culinary Cousins got in since they're in South Carolina."

"Culinary Cousins?" Mark's brows beetled together.

Donna gestured for him to leave. "Go on now. I'll explain later."

Loralee gave an anxious bark as the back door slammed. Janice leaned over the island to locate the sound maker. "New dog?"

"Not really. Loralee is Mark's dog. He just hasn't realized it yet."

A gurgle of laughter brightened Janice's demeanor. "That's a good one."

"No, I mean it. He doesn't understand that he needs this dog more than the dog needs him." Her friend's smirk meant she didn't get it. The crystal plate the shortbread had previously been on was empty with hardly any crumbs left. All her other sweet concoctions were for tonight's mixer. Donna wrinkled her nose. This called for the emergency chocolate, the designer dark chocolate bars she bought in Cincinnati at Findlay's Market. Each decadently delicious bar was ten dollars, but Janice needed it more than she did.

"I thought you were sweet on Mark. Why in the world would you want to pair him up with some ancient dog? Any free time he has will be spent with the dog and not you." She held her hands out as if the whole concept was a no-brainer.

A three-step ladder allowed Donna the extra height she needed to reach the chocolate. She worried about putting the bars up this high, but the cabinet was next to the air conditioning vent. "It's not about time. It's more about creating a home, a sanctuary for the man. He works all the time, takes extra shifts because he has nothing to come home to."

"What about you?"

She turned on the ladder to stare at her friend. "I'm still putting in four twelve-hour shifts at the hospital, then I come here and work. Truthfully, the only time I see Mark is if he drops by for coffee or a dead body shows up in proximity to the inn." Her fingers closed around the elegantly wrapped bars. Still solid, which was a plus.

"Why was he here just now? Coffee, I assume?"

Donna backed down the stepladder carefully, not answering, too concerned about keeping her balance. The last thing she needed was to break something. The inn gobbled up her vacation days, and she hoped to save her sick days for actual emergencies as opposed to broken legs. "Yeah, coffee and an attempt to offload Loralee on me."

"I'd say he succeeded with the dog. At least he's making an effort to see you despite both your busy schedules."

Her lips tilted up at the thought. "It is nice, although his visits usually coincide with food."

"You offer it? He doesn't just open the fridge?"

"Of course he doesn't get into the fridge. I have to lock both it and the pantry to keep out the guests who make themselves too much at home."

Janice stretched her arms above her head and yawned. "I really should be getting back to work. I'm totally booked. When I got that call about Norelle's, I tore out of my kitchen and didn't even put on my shoes."

"Yeah, I noticed the feet. Mark did, too. Are you trying for a reputation as the Barefoot Chef?" She grinned. "Not sure if it's illegal to drive barefoot, but if you're in a wreck, you could be cited for reckless driving."

"Man-made law. Any woman would know it's much more dangerous driving in heels or flip-flops."

Donna unwrapped a bar and pushed it in Janice's direction. "Try that before you go. Got it in Cincinnati."

Her friend popped a square in her mouth and moaned. "Amazing. Are you trying to bribe me or what?"

"No. Can't friends share a chocolate bar together?" There was no way to ease into J.E.'s death. She wasn't even a hundred percent sure the woman was dead. At this point, she was only missing under unusual circumstances. Maybe whoever was driving the car had stolen the purse and car. Enough television dramas had dead peoples' identities confused with someone else. Mark would call her back and give her the details.

"This is your emergency chocolate. No one uses those high cabinets except to store seasonal items or hide something. What's up?" Janice broke off another piece.

"Who called you from Norelle's?" Maria's comment about Janice telling them who to put on the Wall of Death resurrected itself.

"My cousin Eve's son, Jason, is working as a dishwasher at the place. I slipped him a twenty to call me if a new photo went up. I told him I'd give him fifty if he found out who was placing those photos. He called about," Janice looked at her watch, "thirty minutes ago. What do you want to tell me?"

How would she go about bursting her friend's dream of expanding her business? She exhaled long, then inhaled through her nose, trying to think of a kinder, gentler way to say it. Polite, tactful conversation was never her strong point. "I think J. E. is dead."

"Of course she is. I knew that when Jason called. They don't put up a portrait unless it's a sure thing. Think how embarrassing it would be to have to remove it. It would no longer be Norelle's Wall of Death. It would turn into *possibly* dead, rather like that social media site that's always announcing people's deaths who are still alive." Janice slid off the stool, took a sip of her lukewarm coffee, and broke off a sizeable chunk of the candy bar. "This is for the road. These things are addictive. You should stock them and sell them to the guests."

"I couldn't price them high enough to make a profit. They'll have to remain a secret treat."

Janice laughed as she turned to leave. "I know where you hide them."

"Bye now." She didn't bother to verbalize her intent to find a new hiding place, possibly in the cellar where it was always cool and no guests ever roamed.

THE REST OF the day was anticlimactic considering one of her guests may have died. The good news was she didn't die on the premises. It could turn out the woman had an incurable disease. Then again, the woman might walk right through the door any moment now. The front door bell jingled on cue.

Donna hesitated long enough to wash her hands and school her face into an inscrutable expression just in case J.E. was waiting in the foyer. The front entrance remained unlocked during the day to allow guests to come and go as they pleased. Occasionally, potential guests popped in to learn more about the inn.

A stylish, elderly lady stood there, holding the hand of a darling little girl. The two of them could have stepped off a cover of a magazine aimed at upscale grandmothers. *Grandparents who traveled with their grandchildren.* Another demographic she hadn't really gone after. Of course, she wasn't too sure what The Painted Lady had to offer them since they didn't have rooms designed like indoor cabins, water parks, or free children's movies.

"Good afternoon, ladies. What can I do for you?"

The woman gave her a head bob while the little girl's head swiveled as she surveyed her surroundings. "My granddaughter and I are here for the Baptist Missionary Scrapbooking Conference."

"That sounds like fun!" Donna injected as much enthusiasm into her voice as possible. It sounded fake to her. She had no idea what a person did at a missionary scrapbook conference. Did they talk about scrapbooking? Did they make scrapbooks of missionaries or make them for the missionaries?

The woman gave her a stern look, which made her rethink her initial comment. There needed to be a conversational skills conference for B and B owners.

"It's not fun. It's holy work."

Nodding seemed the most appropriate response. She wondered if the woman would eventually whip out a brochure for her to read. "How can I help you?"

"We need a room for the night. The conference hotel is entirely too noisy. There are teenagers roaming the hallways all night and slamming doors."

The little girl piped up. "Grandmother, those were the other attendees. They asked you if you wanted to play Euchre."

There was an empty room. It happened to be close to where the couple was celebrating their second honeymoon, but they were bound to be tired by now since they'd been celebrating all morning. "I do have one upstairs room, but we don't have an elevator."

The look the woman gave her when she mentioned the nonexistent elevator practically froze the blood in her veins. Her granddaughter explained in a clear voice, "Jesus never used an elevator."

Since no electricity or tall buildings existed at that time, she assumed that was a safe bet. She nodded, reminding herself that the ladies would be elsewhere scrapbooking most of the day. They might as well since there was nothing to do while here. Perhaps the third floor might be off-putting. "I could show you the room."

"No need. What's the price?"

This was where the woman would backpedal her way out of here. Many third-party bargain travel sites could lock in hotel rooms for seventy dollars. If you had four hundred rooms to fill, you could charge less. "It's one hundred and eighty due to it being the weekend, but it comes with a gourmet breakfast for both of you. There are plenty of snacks and beverages in the third-floor parlor."

Wait for it. She counted by alligator seconds in her head. By three alligator, the woman was counting out twenty-dollar bills. The granddaughter smiled at Donna before giving her another instructional insight. "Jesus doesn't approve of credit cards."

Another head bob, since there was no way to answer that and not offend the woman who was paying her in cash. "I'll show you to your room. I'm sure you're anxious to get back to the conference."

"In due time. We have to return for our bags, of course, and to inform them the place was much too loud for my tastes. My granddaughter, Scarlett, and I could do with some restorative tea and scones."

Normally, she'd tell a guest that tea in the middle of the day was not an option. She could try to do it, but she didn't think the woman would believe her. "I need your name for the roster. It's per state regulation."

The woman sniffed as if she doubted the regulation part. "Josephina Lee Beujois."

Scarlett arched her eyebrows, a sign she had another important commentary to relate. "Grandmother is related to the famous Son of the South, Robert E Lee."

"I'm sure you're very proud." This time, the little girl bobbed her head.

Donna led the two up the stairs, trying to picture the room, wondering if there was anything to offend. The empty room was more a family suite and contained two beds and a sleeper couch. Most of the pictures were historic landscapes of the area.

Josephina approved of the room, but the tilt of her chin meant the room barely made it. She showed Scarlett the snack pantry area filled with water, sodas, and various nibbles. The concept excited the little girl until her grandmother reminded her that they would wait for a proper meal. She sure hoped Grandmother didn't mean the tea and plundered breakfast pastries she planned to provide. Should she make cucumber sandwiches? She might as well since the woman would probably ask for them.

Ten minutes later, Donna carried the heavy tray upstairs. She planned to heat the water in the parlor microwave to avoid the extra weight and to keep it hot. Her biceps ached as she tightened her grip on the wide tray. The elevator sounded better and better the more she thought about it.

She stifled a groan when she reached the last step as she spotted Scarlett in the parlor. The child might have another insight for her about groaning. Scarlett hustled over to her, bumping Donna's arm in the process. She managed to keep her grip on the tray, but the china slid, jostling each other.

"I want to help. What can I do?"

The young voice reminded her she was dealing with a child, not a pint-sized version of the grandmother. "Pick out the table you want to have tea at. You'll have to sit in the chair for me to know." Donna gave herself a mental pat on the back as Scarlett scurried to a table. She may not have any children, but she could work around them.

The girl sat primly at the table as Donna arranged the plates and cups. "I'm going to make the tea now." She picked up the squat glass pitcher, filled it with water from the wet sink, and placed it in the microwave. "Now, we wait for the water to heat."

"Can you talk to me? My grandmother is lying down with a sick headache. She didn't get any sleep last night with all those church women hopped up on soda and cards."

Donna wondered if she should take the sodas out of the fridge, but the other guests might want them. "So, what do you want to talk about?"

Scarlett placed one finger beside her nose before replying. "What's wrong with buying pre-made paper mattes for pictures? I have a hard time cutting a straight line with the craft scissors."

She should have known the girl would pose a question she knew nothing about. "Scarlett, I don't know anything about scrapbooks. I do know lots of people enjoy making them."

"It's work, hard work. I'm not sure what people enjoy about it."

"Sometimes, when someone really likes something it doesn't seem like work. I wanted to run this inn and there's all types of work, from getting the inn painted to making you tea."

Scarlett's mouth dropped open, making a perfect round O, reminding Donna of the Kewpie dolls that used to be at carnivals.

The microwave bell sounded, preventing a reply. Donna poured the tea into the china teapot. She showed Scarlet the tea infuser and allowed her to pull it through the water, darkening it. The bedroom door opened, and Josephina strode out clutching an ornate cane. The sight of the cane made Donna regret putting the woman on the third floor, but she had chosen the room. The woman's pride would keep her upright, and the stay wouldn't even be twenty-four hours.

"Grandmother, I'm making tea. It's almost ready."

Instead of indulging her grandchild with a smile, Josephina glared at Donna. "Do you think this is wise? The child could burn herself."

Donna detangled Scarlett's fingers from the tea ball and placed the lid on the pot. She worked a crocheted tea cozy over the pot to keep it warm. "Enjoy."

Her long stride allowed her to reach the stairs before any more complaints could reach her. Scarlett struck her as lonely. She wondered what could be done to ease the girl's stay. What she needed was to load up on board games that young people could play during the evenings or on rainy afternoons.

Tennyson's voice carried as she moved toward the kitchen.

"Have you settled in yet? Don't let Donna scare you. She acts tough…"

She was ready to correct the *act* part of the statement, but she decided to wait and hear what else Tennyson had to say. Her grandmother warned her that eavesdroppers never heard good of themselves. All the same, they gathered valuable information about other people.

"But, she has a soft heart under it all. She won't turn you out no matter how much she blusters."

Despite his major, Tennyson showed more wits than she gave him credit for. Her entrance caused the young man to jump back, possibly embarrassed over hugging the elderly dog. People who loved on dogs were decent folks in Donna's mind. A recent news story about an embezzler had one of the victims knowing something wasn't right about the man because his beagle didn't like him.

"We need to get ready for the mixer. First, I'd like to make cupcakes."

"Cupcakes?" Tennyson cocked his head as if he hadn't heard her right.

"Yes, cupcakes. We have a young guest, and I thought it might be appropriate for her."

Tennyson directed a glance at Loralee as if to say I told you so. "Okay. I'll be glad to help."

A tentative tap on the pass-through door sounded before it swung open, revealing the tousled heads of the second honeymooners. The man spoke while the woman managed a hopeful pose with her hands together.

"I noticed a woman and her granddaughter having tea upstairs. I was hoping we could have some, too. We're famished."

Of course they were. They never even came out for breakfast. Before she could decide, the wife added, "We could have it in the dining room. Anything would be fine. Oh, look, dogs!" The woman pushed into the kitchen and knelt beside Jasper and Loralee. "I love dogs."

Tea it was. "I'll bring your tea out, and in about thirty minutes I'll have fresh cupcakes if you want to hang out for that."

The woman had Loralee's head cradled on her lap and was scratching Jasper behind the ears. "Sounds wonderful. I love this place."

Donna smiled as she turned away to fix their tea. People like them were the reason she chose to open the inn. They made her forget about demanding grandmothers and missing food critics, at least for couple of seconds.

Chapter Six

MARIA BREEZED THROUGH the back door as Donna demonstrated how to move around the room offering people appetizers.

"You try." She gave the empty tray to Tennyson.

He held it in his palm, nodding in Maria's direction. "Care for a bite, my lady?" The tray angled as he nodded, sliding off his hand. Maria's quick reflexes caught it before it hit the floor.

"I'm no good at this. Why can't I just do the wine?" Tennyson's pleading gaze swung from Donna to Maria.

Donna could come up with a half dozen reasons why he couldn't pour the wine with the primary one being he wasn't of age. The second would be he'd overfill the glasses. The third…

"Why don't we do the food buffet style the way we usually do?" Maria suggested.

She had a point, a valid one. So far, they hadn't had any issues with people loading their plates down with one type of appetizer, diminishing the supply for everyone else.

"You're right. Then we can put the signs up that warn if something contains seafood, nuts or milk. I was trying to make use of Tennyson's help."

Maria caught her eye as she moved closer. "I'm not sure his skills lie in the waiter area."

The door swung open, and Scarlett stuck her beribboned head in. "Donna, we're back."

Maria motioned to her to come in. "Introduce me to this darling child."

Scarlett slid into the room, keeping close to the wall. Her eyes roamed around the kitchen as Donna talked. "Scarlett, this is my sister-in-law, Maria."

Scarlett offered her hand. "Hello, Maria."

Maria smiled at the greeting and grasped the small hand. "Pleased to meet you…"

Before she could finish, Scarlett yelped. "Dogs! Get them away from me." She dashed for the door, but Tennyson was there first. He dropped to his knees, making himself a little shorter than Scarlett.

Scarlett stopped her anxious efforts to get around Tennyson and listened.

"I used to be afraid of dogs. It made my childhood hard because all my friends had dogs."

"Are you afraid now?"

Tennyson shook his head.

"How did you stop being afraid?"

"It wasn't easy. My parents were allergic to pet dander so we didn't have any pets. Do you have any pets?"

Maria arranged the cold appetizers on the island while Donna iced the remaining cupcakes. They both watched as Tennyson talked Scarlett down from her fright. He eventually had her pet Loralee. The girl left smiling.

"Donna, with that boy's skill set, you could run a day camp," Maria told her. "Maybe something for kids that are afraid of dogs. You already have the dogs."

"Thanks for reminding me." She turned to speak to Tennyson, who was sprawled between the two dogs. "Can you take your canine friends outside while we get the food ready?"

The dogs followed him as if he was a regular pied piper. Maria was right. He had an entirely different skill set.

"What's the deal with the old basset hound?" Maria asked while she arranged the cold appetizers, which she would cover and put back into the fridge.

"Mark brought Loralee by only for the day until he can get her a home. Her owners divorced. Instead of fighting over who gets to keep the dog, they do drive-bys to dump the dog off on the other. As you can tell, Loralee isn't a pet who can easily tolerate their antics. The neighbors couldn't deal with their yelling and called the police. When they discovered a dog was involved, they called Mark."

"That sounds about right. I can't believe they'd have a dog for all that time and just dump her."

"They did. That's not the worst of today." Donna turned the oven on to warm up the fireside popovers, Gorgonzola, hazelnut stuffed mushrooms, and the popular favorite, hot ham and cheese rolls.

"I'm afraid to ask." Maria crinkled her nose. "With you, it's practically movie-of-the-week material."

Donna lowered her voice. "J.E. left this morning on some mission. She hasn't been back. Janice showed up in a state claiming J.E.'s photo was on Norelle's Wall of Death."

"Have you seen it?"

"The picture?"

"Yes."

"No, I'm always afraid to check out the wall because I might see a photo of someone I know. The whole thing is morbid."

Maria brandished an index finger. "It's clever. The bar is in the back. You can't drop in just to see it. You have to make reservations."

"How do they know who is going to die? Do they have black-and-white glossy photographs of celebrities just waiting? J.E. is pretty low profile. How did they even have a photograph of her?"

"Do you know if she's dead?"

"Nada. Nothing. Mark left to investigate an abandoned rental car that could be hers. This is all so weird. It might not be hers or if it is, she might have taken off to start a new life somewhere else. Being one of the most hated people in the restaurant world would have to get old after a while."

"I can see that." Maria agreed readily. "Still, there are other things to consider such as someone wanting her dead. Rumor is she put a halt to more than one culinary career."

Donna used the back of her hand to push the hair out of her eyes. "Janice told me as much when she heard J.E. was heading this way."

"That woman knows everything. I'm going to quit seeing Madame Zelda to have my cards read and just ask Janice." Maria clicked her tongue and poked Donna.

"As for Janice's having some supernatural powers, she doesn't. The Legacy Chamber of Commerce got together some system where they were all writing papers, contacting social media, and what all to get J.E. to visit. It wasn't just The Croaking Frog. It was all of the restaurants."

Maria wrapped the tray in plastic wrap and placed it in the fridge. "I thought Janice didn't want the critic to review her restaurant."

"I thought that too, but she called it a calculated risk. Apparently, Janice did all this research and discovered J.E. had a fondness for gazpacho and set out to make the best ever in hopes J.E. would rave about it."

"Her gazpacho is great. I'd rave about it. So now, no one really knows *anything*." Her sister-in-law emphasized the last word.

"I'm telling you all I know. Janice had me trying to tail the woman, which was a fail as far as following. I cleaned her room, and the woman is neat and tidy."

"Is her luggage still here?"

"Yes, but that doesn't necessarily mean she didn't stage her own disappearance. If she took her luggage, that would look suspicious. Maybe she had extra luggage. Could be she didn't want to take anything from the old life with her." She swallowed, trying to work out the preparations for a new life.

Maria leaned over the island and whispered, "Did you thoroughly clean her room?"

"I just told you. *Oh*." Donna backhanded the overlong bangs that kept getting in her eyes. She'd add *trim bangs* to her to-do list right under *search guest's luggage*. "Mark wouldn't like it."

"He hasn't called and told you not to. Besides, we have latex gloves, and your job is to clean the room. If she never returns, the luggage is yours anyhow."

This was a side of Maria she'd never seen before. Perhaps her sister-in-law shouldn't be the one to handle the billing.

"Come on, Maria, you watch enough cop shows. The police's hands are tied by so many legalities. There could be evidence in the room, even as we speak."

Her fingers picked at the ring on her index finger. Maria made it sound like it was a have-to-do thing, but it wasn't. All she needed was for it to get out that she rifled through a guest's luggage. If the guest was alive or dead made no difference. "It doesn't feel right. What are we looking for anyhow?"

"A motive. Perhaps someone had it in for her. She's bound to know who. Maybe she has an appointment book that tells where she went. A person like her is bound to be paranoid enough to put things in code." Maria pointed at Donna. "You wrote your diary in code because you thought Daniel was reading it."

"Obviously he was, if you know about it. Did he break the code?"

A long pause made Donna suspicious as Maria shook her head. The woman's first loyalty was to her husband. Daniel was no dummy, and the code wasn't hard. "It's okay. Trust me, there was never anything that interesting in my diary. At the time, I thought Jeff McCormick lending me a pencil in math class meant something. I realize my habit of overanalyzing everything created relationships that did not exist. For a brief time, I wondered if Jeff would be hurt if I chose not to take the McCormick name. I didn't want to spend my entire life explaining b*ig M little C big C* when it came to my last name."

"The boy was thrown over for a difficult last name?"

"He wasn't thrown over. He was never ever interested in me. I only imagined he was, which is pretty much what you're doing with evidence in the suitcase and coded date book stuff." Her cheeks rounded as she blew out a long breath. Here she thought Maria was the functionally sane one in the family.

"We'll agree to talk after the mixer. By then, you may have changed your mind. I'll still be here if we need to tidy up."

Tennyson burst into the room. "Scarlett's grandmother wants to talk to you, and she's hot, not in a good way. It would be creepy if she was, because she's old and…"

Great. The day had a few more slap-downs to deliver. Donna slowly enunciated the words. "What did you say?"

"What did I say? Um…" He scratched his cheek. "I'm not sure. She came by and asked me if the mangy dogs were mine. I told her no because they weren't."

"Not sure why that would have upset her. Anything else?"

His hand rubbed across his chin. "I asked her if she was going to the wine mixer tonight?" His voice winged up a little near the end of the sentence, making it into a question.

"Got it." She held up a thumb to Tennyson, who breathed a noticeable sigh of relief.

A firm knock sounded on the pass-through door. "Miss Donna, I need to talk to you."

"Come in." She already knew how she'd defuse the situation. The woman had her hands balled on her hips and her eyes narrowed in outrage, but before she could speak, Donna did. "I'm sure you're very tired after your conference. I thought I'd bring you dinner up to your room. Free of charge, of course."

"What would dinner be?"

"Stuffed chicken breast along with a salad. I could make soup and sandwiches if you prefer that. Maria can find you a DVD player and a nice Disney movie, too."

"Really?" The woman actually looked pleased. "How nice. I prefer the earlier movies such as *Snow White* or *Cinderella*."

Maria shot a confused look toward Donna before replying, "On it."

Josephina left, perhaps slightly chagrined. She never got to fight the battle she'd prepared to fight. All the same, she'd won in some bizarre fashion.

"Obi-Wan Kenobi, tell me where I'm getting these movies and the DVD player?"

"My mother, of course. The woman has the Disney princess movies. Let me call her and she'll probably deliver them." There was also the chance her mother would want to stay and help. As Janice would say, it was a calculated risk.

"I'm surprised you're working so hard to please that woman. It's not like you to give away things free."

"I'm doing it more for the granddaughter. I can't imagine how it must be for her if her grandmother foams at the mouth whenever she comes across something she doesn't like or approve of. I can't imagine what life must be like if using an elevator is a sin."

Maria murmured an agreement as she tidied up the island. "Don't forget to call your mom. She's been waiting for a chance to visit ever since you purchased the inn."

"Ah, she may have mentioned it." As tempting as an eye roll was, she fought it, knowing Maria might mention it to Daniel, who would tell their mother. Cecilia Tollhouse's petite height and delicate features fooled people into thinking she was some fragile flower who always needed help. Family friends mistakenly thought she'd deferred to her husband. She hadn't. Most people thought a mother was the heart of the family, but in theirs, she was the engine.

Daniel had hinted that Mother would like to help, but Donna knew that even at seventy-two years, Cecilia would attempt to do everything her way. It didn't mean her way was wrong. Looking back, her father followed her advice from where to vacation to when to move. Cecilia Tollhouse even told her husband what stocks to invest in, which had worked out well for Donna since her inheritance enabled her to buy the inn. She might as well suck it up and call.

The phone rang once. A breathless voice announced, "Cici here."

Who was Cici? Her brow furrowed. She'd called the right number. Her family had had the same number for the last thirty years. She should know it. "Mom?"

"Ah, Donna. It's unusual for you to call."

The guilt screws tightened. "I know. Sorry for not calling. I hate to ask, but I need a favor."

A light laugh sounded in her ear. "Of course you do or you wouldn't have called."

The woman excelled in everything she did, but she'd put Cecilia Tollhouse against any mother as far as inspiring guilt. "There's a grandmother here with her granddaughter."

Her mother made some light sighing noise. "What a blessing grandchildren are."

Her initial response would have been to say how would you know, you've never had any, but that would play into her hands. This wasn't the first time the subject of grandchildren had come up. Ever since she'd graduated from nursing school, she'd heard some reference to it. When she hit forty, her mother, not a progressive thinker, did not consider Donna as a potential mother anymore. Instead, she shifted to the idea that perhaps one of her male patients might be a single parent. Whenever a too friendly male patient showed up on her ward, she wondered if the man was a plant. Her mother was capable of superhuman feats of manipulation.

"Yes, but sometimes they get bored. I was wondering if you could bring some of the older princess movies and the DVD player. It would give the little sweetheart something to do."

"I'd love to do that."

Her ready acceptance relaxed Donna's tight shoulders. That was one less thing to worry about. "See you soon."

Her mother's voice took on a wheedling tone. "Tonight's your mixer, isn't it?"

"Yes, it is." She wondered how her mother knew since she had changed it from Friday to Saturday. Maria made a fast pivot and

KILLER REVIEW | 73

headed for the dining room. "That's why I thought the movie would be nice."

"Good thinking. Would business casual be appropriate dress?"

Now it starts. As much as she didn't want her mother at the mixer, it would be the equivalent of trying to stop a mudslide already in progress. Her mother charmed everyone. The people were unaware her mother was moving them in a direction that best suited her. "Anything you wear will be wonderful."

"Kiss, kiss." Cecilia added a smacking sound.

Donna could never bring herself to do something so corny. "Love you."

Maria peeked back in the kitchen. "Is it safe to come back in yet?"

It wasn't too hard to figure out who was responsible for the information leak. How often did her mother and Maria speak? Obviously, it was more than she did. As a kid, her mother was a loving Madonna-like figure who would go all mad dog if anything threatened her family. Now, as a person of perspective—how she liked to refer to being fifty, almost fifty-one—her mother puzzled her.

"When I called her, she answered the phone as Cici. Do you know what's up with that?"

"That's her special dating name."

Her eyelids fluttered on their own, similar to butterflies caught in a strong wind. *Dating?* She had to have heard wrong. As a nurse, Donna expected the knees to go first, after spending years on the hard cement floors, not the hearing. "Dating name?"

"Her friend, Marlene, came up with it. I think she used to go by it when she was a child. Anyhow, Marlene thinks a woman should never give out her real name, in case the guy turns out to be a dud. It makes it harder for them to track down a woman. Most of the men don't use their real names either."

"Alrighty then. How do you know if whomever you're talking to isn't a liar and a cheat?"

Maria wrinkled her nose. "How long has it been since you've been on a date?"

"It depends. I guess when I went out with Arnie in an attempt to trap the killer doesn't count. It has been a few years."

"Things are different now. Unfortunately, people sign up for online dating while in a relationship. I guess they want to see what is out there before taking the plunge. On the other hand, it just means you get someone who would cheat on you since he's done it before."

"Ugh. No wonder I don't date." She pulled out the cookie sheet and covered it with parchment paper before placing the frozen ham and cheese rolls on it. Being alone wasn't in her long-term plans, but she kept missing the prime time to meet someone. It sounded as if the people on dating sites were already in a relationship, which didn't bode well.

"I'm not so sure about that."

The comment caused her to almost drop the pan she was sliding into the oven. A suspicion climbed up her spine reminiscent of one of those strange movie monsters that burst out of someone's body when the dramatic music pauses. "Maria, you didn't, did you?"

Chapter Seven

THE OVEN BUZZER chirped the same time the front door bell jingled. Any curiosity Donna had about her potential visitor was answered by a sing-song statement.

"Mother's here to save the day!"

That was another thing about her maternal parent. The woman felt the need to tweak everything that wasn't working to her specification. Maybe she could use that trait to her advantage and get Cecilia in a conversation with Grandmother Grumpy, but when push came to shove, she had no doubt the grandmother could pick up her featherweight mother and toss her out the window.

The kitchen door opened as Cecilia barged in carrying a large shallow box. "Oh. Maria's here."

Somehow, her mother made it sound like it was a party and everyone had been invited but her. "Yes, she is. I'm sure you knew that."

"Possibly." She placed the box on the table and unpacked the DVD player and movies, causing some papers to flutter to the floor.

Donna reached for them, noticing they had snapshots with catchy taglines such as *Looking for My Last First Date* or *Come, Fly Away with Me*. They must be her mother's potential dating prospects. Daniel and she had always expected her mother to remarry since she was happiest supervising others. There had to be plenty of men who would enjoy being lovingly directed by an attractive senior citizen. A quick glance at the profiles informed her that they were all retired and considered themselves financially comfortable. All good. One was obsessed with golf, the other with being out on the lake with his boat, and the third one wanted to travel the world.

"Mother, I think any one of these men would be a good date for you."

Her mother giggled, patted her on the shoulder, but refused to take the papers back. "Oh no, sweetie, those are for you. I had so many replies to my profile I couldn't date or talk to them all. I decided to share my wealth. Just think how excited they'll be hearing from a tall blonde who's twenty years younger. You'll be their dream come true."

Maria put her hand over her mouth, trying to hide her amusement, but her eyes still twinkled. At least someone was enjoying this. "Mother, I'm not into dating right now."

"How well I know. Give up on that detective. Daniel told me he moves as slow as molasses in January."

Daniel, too? She mouthed the words to Maria, who blushed but was unwilling to rat out her husband. Was there no one not talking about her love life or lack of one? Her mother wanted to share her romantic picks with her. Did it get any worse?

"Thanks, Mother. Let me show you where Scarlett and her grandmother are staying. You can deliver the DVD player and even hook it up for them." Her mother followed her out the door. Donna pointed up the stairs since she didn't have time to run up them. Cecilia repeated the room number back to her, proving she had the right one and wouldn't knock on random doors and start invasive conversations with her guests.

By the time she returned to the kitchen Daniel and Maria had their heads together and were laughing. It didn't take a genius to figure out what had caused their merriment. "Daniel Tollhouse, I did not appreciate you throwing me under the mother bus."

Her brother managed a sheepish grin. "She was on me about grandchildren. You know how she can be. No harm is done because she'll never meet Mark."

Of course, the good detective's impromptu visits might occur while her mother was in the house. Thinking of the possibility felt as if a movie monster had just sunk all eighteen claws into her, enough to have her pounding her head against the wall. It could only get worse if Maria shared her plan to snoop through the missing critic's luggage. The prospect had Donna grinding her back molars.

"You owe me." Donna directed the comment at her brother. "You aren't staying?"

"No, I only stopped by to greet my loving wife. I have a couple hours of paperwork to sort through."

"That can wait. Take Mother out to dinner. She'd love it." It would also get her out of the inn.

Cecilia had the door half-opened and overheard the plan. "Daniel, how nice to see you." Her mother gestured with her manicured fingers. "Looks like the whole family is here."

"Oh, Daniel dropped by to see Maria and take you out to dinner." No way would she allow her mother to pretend everyone was asked to the inn except her, even if it was true.

"That's so sweet." She smiled at Daniel, but cut her eyes to Donna.

Her mother was no intellectual lightweight. No one could out-manipulate her either. Donna may have thought her years with egotistical doctors placed her in good stead, giving her valuable experience, because they never expected those under them to be as smart or smarter than them. Cecilia, on the other hand, never underestimated her opponent.

"Children," she addressed all of them, making Donna feel about ten. "I've been so busy going out with all these wonderful men I'm dinner-ed out. Besides, I have to be on my game the entire time. I welcome an evening here, where I can relax and be myself."

The *being herself* might be the problem. People usually loved her mother, despite her offering them advice as if they were blood relatives. By night's end, she'd give Donna detailed suggestions on the décor, food, and even what she should be wearing. Although, since her mother had impeccable taste, there would be some noteworthy ideas. Which would make it all that much more annoying.

"That's a shame. I'd really like to take you out, but another time. I wouldn't want your suitors getting jealous seeing you out with a young man."

Her brother was laying it on thick. Her mother simpered and coyly dipped her head as if she were sixteen instead of seventy-two.

"That's no issue. I went out with a gentleman who was fifty-four this week."

Donna's eyebrows shot up so high she must have moved her hairline up an inch. "Mother!" Did she even know this woman anymore?

"No worries about having a stepfather near your age. All the man wanted to talk about was investments, particularly investing my money. I wouldn't be surprised if he uses the dating site to drum up new clients. The man was much too dull for you or me. That's why I didn't include his profile with the ones I gave you."

"Profiles?" Daniel inquired, with much more interest than she wanted.

She rounded the island to reach her brother and gave him a slight shove. "You need to go. You have work to do. Remember paperwork? Kiss your wife goodbye and go." She gave another shove for good measure.

The man had the nerve to laugh, slipped away from her, kissed his wife, then headed for the door. "Maria, I want a full report when you get home."

She cringed a little thinking of Maria and Daniel discussing their upcoming midnight jaunt into the missing woman's bedroom. Oh, wait, he knew nothing about that. She rubbed one hand over her face. At least something was going right.

"All right, ladies, we need to swing into gear and get the dining room ready."

Maria and Cecilia ducked into the dining room. Tennyson entered from the back entrance in pressed jeans and a black T-shirt with a tuxedo printed front. It was a definite step up from his "Testimony is a valid form of epistemic justification—just take my word for it" shirt. People didn't like slogans that made them think or might even imply the wearer was smarter than they were.

"You're looking sharp. Any special reason?" Most of her day felt like being in a house of mirrors. Nothing was ever what she thought it was. The fact she could start over tomorrow with a new day served as a long-awaited gift.

"Um, yeah." His eyes shifted as his hand reached up to touch his nose.

On one of those BBC mystery shows she liked so much, such behavior was indicative of lying, but Tennyson hadn't said anything yet. On the other hand, he could have a touch of attention deficit disorder. Those with it had a hard time maintaining eye contact. She gestured with her oven-mitted hands for him to continue.

"I noticed whenever you have a mixer that Herman shows up."

She pulled the lightly toasted ham and cheese rolls out of the oven. "That he does."

"I figured Winnie would be lonely in that house all by herself. I may have invited her."

He was so transparent, which meant he'd be a terrible salesperson or politician. It was cute in a way. "It's the only polite thing to do," Donna agreed, "but before you invite anyone else, ask first. As you know, I make only so much food, and I have to factor in how many people will be here."

A wide smile stretched across his narrow face, making him almost handsome. Hopefully, Herman's granddaughter would have the common decency to be polite to her normally morose helper. A smitten Tennyson was right up there with her mother dating. *Please God, save her from any other weirdness tonight.*

"No worries. She'll hardly eat anything, being a girl and all."

Donna snorted at that one. She could remember her own mother making her eat before a date so she wouldn't eat too much. It made no sense, but maybe men were looking for the lightest eater, hoping it meant a smaller grocery bill. Although nowadays, most women would be paying the grocery bill to ensure they didn't have a steady diet of fish sticks, chicken wings, and pizza. Good food cost money.

The iconic ring of a rotary phone echoed in the foyer. Donna almost forgot she had a landline since the bookings and inquiries came through the website. It really was a necessity for any business, which is the reason she put it in. No one answered it, forcing Donna to pull the canapes out of the oven and jog down the hall.

"Hello."

"Jane?" A male voice made the name into the question.

Donna realized her mistake immediately. She'd forgot to identify the inn. "This is The Painted Lady Inn. Whom did you wish to speak to?"

"She told me she'd be staying there."

Jane. She flipped open the roster located by the phone. *Jane Ellen Muscovy.* "Yes, yes, she is, but she's not here right now. Could I take a message?" A pause followed her request, then she heard the sound of a disconnection. Donna stood staring at the phone receiver as her mother passed by and clicked her tongue.

"You wouldn't have to wait around for your detective to call if you contacted one of those men whose profile I gave you. They're all retired and have plenty of time to wait on you. Not like that policeman who's always running here and there but never has time to take you out to a dinner you didn't make."

Donna hung up the phone with a clump. A half-turn shielded her face from the discerning eyes of her mother. How much did the woman know? She couldn't put it all on Daniel and Maria. Her mother had an extensive network of friends and associates. Just because she refused to share information didn't mean her mother didn't have other sources, accurate sources it seemed.

"It's mixer time." She gave her mother a hopeful look. "Would you like to be a wine steward tonight?"

Her mom clapped her hands together as if offered a shopping spree instead of a job. "Oh, that sounds like fun. Do I get to act all snobby? Say things like this is a full-bodied red with a playful finish?"

Her simple delight made it easy to see why men might be enchanted with her mother. "You could say that if you wanted, but just ask people if they want white or red wine. Then you give them a small or tall pour. The glasses are big so even a tall pour is half a glass. In the end, no one gets more than three glasses. You have to be vigilant. Some will try to help themselves. You will be the official keeper of the wine."

"Got it." She snapped a two-finger salute. "I'll be the wine sergeant."

"It's steward."

Cecilia gave an airy wave. "Whatever. Can I have a tall pour, too?"

Geesh. Who knew the major work of running an inn would include managing her family. "We all can after the mixer, except for Tennyson who isn't twenty-one. I'll have Tennyson bring up the bottles you need from the cellar."

"Why did you hire that young man to help you when your mother could have done the same thing without the expense of live-in help?" Cecilia's tight expression couldn't be blamed on Botox.

Donna considered some sad story about Tennyson being an orphan but knew good and well the boy would spill the facts. Honesty sometimes worked. Maybe it might this time. "The inn is such a big undertaking. It's more work than I thought it would be. In the beginning, it was hard physical work."

"You didn't think I was strong enough." She placed both hands on her hips, looking more like a twelve-year-old than the Valkyrie warrior she knew her mother to be. The offended look reminded her that her mother didn't mind playing dirty.

"You were grieving. I didn't think it would be a good time to ask for help."

"It would have been the perfect time. It would have gotten my mind off how alone I was and destined to spend my golden years as a third wheel with some other couples. That isn't always pleasant. No matter how close the friend, they assume I'm out to steal the husband."

"You'd never do such a thing."

Her mother gave a superior sniff. "None of them had husbands worth stealing." Cecilia chuckled at Donna's indrawn breath. "Your father was a rare man. I don't expect to replace him, ever. All the same, I wouldn't mind going out to the theater, dinner, or even play a game of golf with a gentleman companion."

"Ah," She scrambled for a right response. It was difficult because she didn't expect a simple request for a children's movie to result in a soul-baring session. "I'd like for you to enjoy yourself."

"Good. Invite me over more to help. I have a flair for the hospitality thing." She wrinkled her nose—as close to a smirk as her mother ever allowed herself—then walked into the kitchen, calling for Tennyson.

Donna darted back into the kitchen, praying her hot appetizers hadn't become lukewarm. If so, she'd give them a few minutes in the warmer oven. The mixer should go well since she had more help than she usually had and three fewer guests to serve. Donna stopped short and cringed, realizing she had forgotten about dinner for Grandmother Grumpy and Scarlett.

TWO AND HALF hours later, Donna, Cecilia, Maria, and Tennyson were gathered around the butcher block island, nibbling on the leftover hor d'oeuvres. The small number of nibbles left caused some grumbling among the group.

Donna couldn't resist teasing Tennyson. "I thought you told me Winnie ate like a bird."

"A condor, maybe" Maria added, before he could defend his love.

"I didn't say bird. I think I said she wouldn't eat much. Obviously, she was hungry." He cast a forlorn glance at the almost empty platter.

The timer beeped. Donna turned, opened the oven door, and lifted out a tray of hot appetizers. "I couldn't let my helpers go hungry."

A spontaneous cheer sounded as she used the metal spatula to move the treats to the platter. She placed the cookie sheet in the industrial-sized sink. Knowing what could happen at the mixer, she'd also kept back a plate of cold appetizers, desserts, and a chilled bottle of Moscato. She placed a bottle of soda in front of Tennyson. "Here's yours."

She ignored his groan as she opened the wine for the three of them. "Do we have anything left from the mixer?"

"Half a bottle of an acceptable Malbec," her mother replied, as she lifted her filled wine glass, staring at it with deep affection.

"I hope you didn't offer it to the guests like that."

"Of course not, but Malbec has never been my favorite even though it's on the upswing in popularity now. I simply asked if they wanted red or white."

A phone chirp had Tennyson looking at his phone, grinning, and then bidding them goodbye.

Normally, she'd grumble about him getting out of work, but she needed to get everyone gone so she could inspect J.E.'s luggage. She'd expected Mark to call by now. Maybe her mother was right about getting out and meeting men, although she preferred any contenders to be on the right side of fifty-five. She spent enough of her time indulging whiny male patients. She didn't intend to spend the rest of her life as a private nurse.

Maria tossed back her wine similar to doing shots at the local dive. "Let's get these dishes done so we can investigate."

Surely, she didn't say that. Donna's mouth dropped open. She shot her hands through her hair, hoping her mother hadn't heard. While she had her own doubts about the legality of searching a guest's room, she didn't need her mother to lecture her. Besides, she'd read in some travel magazine that maids went through belongings all the time, often curious about their guests. Some even paraded around in the guest's clothes and lingerie.

"What investigation, Maria?"

Cecilia's cool inquiry let Donna know her mother didn't miss a thing. Her sister-in-law shot her an anguished look. Donna waited three alligators' worth. Nope, no great answers came to mind. "We have a missing guest, the food critic, J.E. Muscovy."

"She's wicked," her mother interjected, but tacked on in case she didn't know exactly what she meant, "But I love her reviews. She pulls no punches. No one has to guess how she feels about something. Why is she missing?"

"That's a good question." She blew out a long breath, doubting if it were wise to mention any of this to her mother whose gossip network rivaled Janice's. "She left this morning after telling Daniel she was going to A Little Bit of Paris. Janice called me and asked me to tail her since she wanted to know if she would visit The Croaking Frog."

Cecilia rubbed her hands together. "This already sounds like one of those mysteries that lady detective solves every week on Snoop Network."

"Anyhow, I never caught up with her since I got pulled over for speeding. She was driving a white car. By the time I got to the café the morning rush was over. An employee told me she may have been there, but it's hard to say with so many non-locals looking alike."

Her mother prompted her. "Go on." She filled her own glass with the acceptable Malbec she must have retrieved from the dining room.

"Nothing really. I came back to clean the rooms. J.E.'s was neat and tidy with a sticky note of restaurant names on the floor. There was a black line drawn through Sylvester's."

Maria held up a finger, halting her recitation. "What does that mean?"

"I'm clueless. It could mean she was going to review it or that she already had. Janice showed up the same time Mark got a call. She was upset that J.E.'s photo had gone up on Norelle's Wall of Death."

Cecilia clicked her tongue. "We all know that poor woman is dead, then. No one goes up on the wall unless they're dead. What's this about Mark being here? Was he investigating?"

Leave it to her mother to pick up on that part of the story. "He stops by occasionally for coffee."

Maria was on the receiving end of a significant look from her mother-in-law. Seriously, her own family was spying on her. "Mark got a call. The police found a white car that may be the one J.E. Muscovy was driving. I'm waiting to hear back."

"Anything else?"

The way her mother asked reminded her of when she'd been caught in a lie as a child. Her mother never accused her of lying. She kept asking if there was anything else until she confessed all. Lying was not a skill Donna ever perfected.

"There was a phone call when you saw me in the hall."

"You were holding the phone and had that thousand-yard stare. Who was on the phone?"

"I have no clue. It was a man who asked for Jane. He said Jane told him she'd be staying here. When I asked for a message, he hung up." If something had happened to J.E, if there were a perpetrator, he wouldn't bother to call and risk exposure. Something was going on, but she had no clue what it was. A chill pebbled her skin. Her grandmother would call it someone *walking over her grave*. The saying never made much sense because she wasn't in the grave yet.

"Maria thought we might find something in her luggage. As the owner, I can go into the room without a search warrant. If there is something worth finding, I can pass on the information."

Her mother slapped her hands together three times. "All right, ladies, we have a case to solve. Anyone have latex gloves?"

Chapter Eight

WHERE WAS THE lecture Donna expected about doing the right thing? Maria shot her a confused gaze and shrugged her shoulders. Her mother, Cecilia, beamed. "I can't wait." She rubbed her bare hands together. "I thought after your father died there would never be any fun or adventure in my life again, with nothing left but a bland march to the grave."

Donna hadn't even decided if she should go through the missing woman's possessions. Her mother made it sound like the remedy for grieving widowhood. It was hard to tell if anticipation or determination flared in Cecilia's eyes. If she told her mother no, it wouldn't stop the woman from coming back in cat burglar black to do her own investigation. A guest would probably call the police. If Mark found out, it would take more than a pot roast to patch up things. He couldn't arrest her for going into her own room, but her mother was a different matter.

"This is an almost full inn. There will be no spy movie antics. We clean up the kitchen, giving everyone plenty of time to settle down for the night. I'll get my cinnamon rolls started so they can rise. Then we proceed into the bedroom after locking the front door. It wouldn't serve any of us if J.E. came waltzing in and found us in her room."

Her mother shook her head. "The woman's portrait is on The Wall of Death."

"True." Maria held up one finger. "How do we even know the woman staying at the inn is J.E.? Until now, I didn't know if J.E. was a man or woman. Maybe this is some huge scam."

"Could you debate *and* clean?" Donna reached for her recipe book, even though she knew the cinnamon rolls recipe almost by heart. Guests always commented on the warm, comforting smell of hot rolls when they came down in the morning. While she liked to change up the menu, she had to keep the rolls along with the tollhouse cookies. It was part of the brand.

Her mother's voice carried. "J.E has to be a woman simply because of the reviews. No man uses such extensive vocabulary."

"Are you saying men don't know many words?" Maria's retort carried over the noise of the dishwasher.

The guests should all be ensconced in their beds, watching television, or engaging in an equally loud activity. Jasper, who was stuck in the cellar, began barking. Loralee joined in with a long bay. Tennyson had forgotten the dogs, but she had, too.

Her mother stopped talking, sprinted to the cellar, and swung open the door. The hounds bounded up the stairs and into the kitchen.

"Am I the grandmother to two granddogs now?"

A wondrous, devious idea took form. "Loralee, the basset hound, is a victim of a broken home. Her owners divorced, but neither one will take the dog. They keep dumping her on the other in the middle of the night, causing quite a ruckus. She's hanging out here until she can be taken to the animal shelter."

Maria gave her a questioning stare which Donna decided to ignore. "Yeah, it's sad. Since she's an old dog, no one will want her." Her eyes teared up as she thought of Loralee in a too small kennel.

"Why can't you take her?" Her mother posed the same question

Mark had asked her.

"There are guests who don't like dogs or are allergic to them. I already have some issues with Jasper. I try to keep him out of the common areas as much as possible. With two dogs, they could run through the house, possibly tripping guests. There's not much I can do for the old gal. Could you take the dogs out for me?"

Her mother shepherded the dogs out the door with some tongue clicking that dogs responded to better than their own names.

"That was a work of art. Cecilia will be making Loralee her own by tomorrow," Maria whispered.

"Yep, I outmaneuvered the manipulator. I wonder if that makes me officially an adult."

"It may be exactly what your mother needs—someone to fuss over as opposed to endless dates. We don't even know if these men are all on the level."

"I could ask Mark to run a background check on them."

The back door thumped shut, followed by dog nails on the linoleum. "I heard you. Don't bother. All the men I went out with had background checks. Your mother isn't a naïve teenager."

"Of course not." It was hard to know what to say when gossiping about her mother's love life.

The subject didn't faze her mother, who slapped her on the back. "Get a move on those rolls, we got work to do."

CECILIA HAD SOMEHOW taken the lead on the room investigation. "Ladies, we need to take our shoes off before proceeding."

Donna almost refused just because it felt like her mother was in charge, and her goal was to look as normal as possible if caught in the act. One look at Maria's platform shoes, however, had her toeing her own slip-ons off her feet. Every time Maria stepped on the hardwood surface, it would be a loud clomp. Any of the guests could trace their movements down the hall and into the bedroom.

The three of them donned latex gloves. Donna kept her apron on while Maria pulled her hair into a bun. Cecilia tucked a pencil behind her ear and carried a cleaning caddy.

After opening the door with the passkey, Maria and Donna closed the blinds and drapes. She convinced her mother against the use of flashlights, which would appear somewhat criminal from the outside. The neighbors already harbored doubts about her and needed no further ammunition.

The room smelled fresh due to lemony furniture polish and the mint-scented bathroom cleaner. There really wasn't anything to search. Cecilia immediately went to the dresser and opened and closed drawers in a rapid fashion.

"Mother, please. We're trying to be covert about this. Don't slam things around."

Her mother pinned her with one of those looks, the one that said, "I'm your mother, and I know what you're doing." This time, she didn't.

"You act like you expect that woman to walk right through the door."

Her gaze went to the door, not totally convinced it hadn't moved a centimeter. Might as well lock it, just to be safe.

Maria held up a red, sexy nightie. The bra cups had a bit of red film hanging from them. "It's brand new. Still has the price tag on it."

Cecilia darted over to look at the price. She whistled, resulting in the dogs barking in the distance. Donna leaned against the wall, wondering why she ever thought this was a workable plan. Maria came up with the idea, not that she wouldn't have considered it. She, however, would be much more low-key. It reminded her of the saying about how two people could keep a secret if one of them was dead. There was no way both her mother and Maria would keep their mouths shut.

Her eyes closed as she pictured the conclusion of tonight's snooping. Daniel would ask Maria what took her so long. Then, she'd gleefully inform him she'd been part of a deep-cover investigation into the missing guest. Never mind that the deep cover meant *tell no one*. Her brother would raise an eyebrow and mentally blame her for leading his wife down the garden path of possibly criminal activities under the sleuthing heading. No way would he consider Maria came up with the idea.

Good heavens, who would her mother tell? She might even write about it on her blog, *Still Sane after Seventy*. Considering some of her recent behavior, that might be debatable, too. This would not turn out well.

"I found a notebook!" Maria spoke the words only a few decibels below shouting level. Donna prayed the guests had their televisions blasting. At least there was no one on this floor and no reason to creep downstairs since the snack pantries were full.

Her mother gave her a shove as she moved past her. "For Pete's sake, open your eyes and quit that groaning. We're trying to help you."

Help her? She hadn't asked for their assistance. She'd already checked the room—within acceptable housekeeping guidelines. Maria brandished the stenographer's notebook and flipped it open. Her eager expression melted.

"What is it?" What would be anticlimactic after finding a sought-after clue? "Recipes?"

"No." Maria motioned Donna closer. "I think this is your area of expertise. It's in code or a foreign language." She held up one finger. "Before you ask, it's not Spanish."

She took the notebook filled with an occasional letter or sign, but it didn't resemble any of the simple numerical codes that obviously hadn't fooled her brother in the past. "I'm no cryptographer."

Her mother plucked the book out of her hand. The woman had the attitude there wasn't an obstacle she couldn't conquer. The sound of page turning filled the room.

"Seriously, quit pretending to read. If we can't figure it out…"

"Hush." Her mother shook a warning finger that made Donna go silent. Cecilia kept flipping pages and would gasp occasionally, then turn another page. She must be reading because her eyes were going back and forth. Her mother wouldn't welcome another interruption from her, so she elbowed Maria to ask any pertinent questions.

Message taken, she leaned over her mother-in-law's shoulder to peer at the notebook. "What language is it?"

Her mother glanced up. "Shorthand. I used to be a secretary before I married. So few people know shorthand anymore that it's become a dead language, like Latin." Her brow furrowed as if contemplating something deep. "No, make that Greek since we still use Latin in medicine and in common prefixes and suffixes."

"Mom, what does it say?" If not stopped, Cecilia Tollhouse would launch into an impromptu language lesson.

"Mmm, your guest was a very conflicted woman. It feels wrong telling her innermost secrets."

"Duh, you just read her secrets. Maria handled her lingerie. I'm not sure we can get much creepier. Besides, there may be important information inside the notebook relating to her disappearance, or possible death."

Cecilia paged back in the notebook and reread a few lines. "I can tell you this much, this is not a woman who planned on dying just yet. She had a whole new life planned for herself. A real bucket list type of thing."

Typical. Her mother always gave out information in dribs and drabs. She used to print out informational tidbits about their family vacation and place them by their cereal bowls until someone guessed the location. Donna had always deciphered the clues before anyone else. It may have sharpened her detective skills. Still, no one had time for this. She made a grab for the book, pulling it from her mother's hand.

It definitely was shorthand. It could have been hieroglyphics from as much as she understood. "Okay, you got me. Tell me what's in it. I'll know if I should hint to Mark to search the room. He'd do it normally. After searching for clues the police are obligated to turn over her possessions to the next of kin if she has any. At least I think they do."

Her mother snatched back the notebook. "Would I be brought in as a special shorthand expert?" Cecilia's chin went up at that stubborn angle her father referred to as her snapping turtle stance. Everyone knew snapping turtles didn't let go until it thundered. And there was no rain in the forecast.

"Come on. That would indicate we'd been in the room and knew she had a shorthand notebook. Besides, there might not be anything in it that's important." She knew it was a mistake the moment she suggested calling her mother for those movies. Why hadn't she listened to her gut? This is what happens when you turned to a blood relative for assistance. There was always a price to pay.

"There's lots of goodies in this book. I only read part of it. Allow me to say it would blow the lid off restaurant reviewing. I may never believe another one again." She used the book to fan herself.

Maria broke first, grabbing Cecilia's arm. "Tell us!" She glanced at her watch. "It's after eleven. In ten more minutes, your son will either call the police or drive over here. Then we'll have to explain to him what we're doing. I don't want to do that. There are some things men don't understand."

Her argument didn't make sense to Donna, but her mother bobbed her head in agreement. Why J.E. recorded everything in a notebook puzzled her, but it was safer than a computer that could easily be hacked, especially if it belonged to the newspaper conglomerate that published her reviews.

"Let's sit, girls." Her mother plopped down on the bed and patted the space beside her. Donna and Maria didn't need any more encouragement. Cecilia opened the book to the first page.

"Jane is losing her sense of taste due to radiation therapy she'd had to treat throat cancer. The cancer was cured, but her job is in jeopardy. She no longer feels confident to judge cuisine. Lately, she hasn't been as rough of a reviewer as previously."

Donna tried to remember the last review she'd read. Some hole-in-the-wall French restaurant where she praised both the smoked duck and the vichyssoise. "I hadn't noticed that until you mentioned it. She complimented the entrée and the soup in her last review. She did call the asparagus limp, but that's self-evident."

"Wait." Maria held up her hand. "She came here to commit suicide because she could no longer do her job!"

"No," Donna hissed. "Get that thought out of your head. People do not come to The Painted Lady Inn to commit suicide." After the last murder incident, Mark had managed to get them to not print the name of the inn in the article since the reporter was his nephew. The detective may have mentioned leaving his Harley to him in his will to accomplish it.

Maria straightened her shoulders as she looked over Cecilia. "I didn't say that, but you have to admit whenever someone dies in Legacy in an unusual manner the inn is connected somehow."

"Coincidence."

"The inn isn't involved, according to Jane."

Both Maria and Donna spoke in unison. "What?"

Cecilia paused for a moment and then showed the page. "It says here the trip was sprung on her at the last moment. The scrapbook conference had already taken every room, except here."

"What else does it say?" The confident, demanding woman she met was far from suicidal. That meant she had a plan. "Why Legacy?"

"The corporation and her agent wanted her to come down here and skewer some chefs. They even handpicked four."

The orange sticky note with the names resting on the bedside table drew her attention. "What about Sylvester's Salon?"

Her mother gave her a suspicious look. "Are you sure you can't read shorthand?"

"If I could, I wouldn't be sitting here listening to the annotated version of the journal."

Her mother patted her hand. "Always the speed demon. Well, the paper decided she should write a vicious review of his restaurant. Bad reviews sell papers. As you know, the newspaper business hasn't been doing that well lately, not with people getting their news from social media."

Donna sucked in her lips. Why hadn't she taken shorthand in high school? "I bet the part about the newspapers going out of business isn't in the journal."

"It's still true." She flipped to the next page. "Sylvester's real name is George. Surprisingly, they went to chef school together. Just think, Jane was training to be a chef. She doesn't explain why she never became one."

Maria interrupted Cecilia's desire to journey down another path. "Were George and the reviewer friends way back then?"

"Ha! Friends you say. The type with *benefits*." Her mother emphasized the last word and winked at them as if they might not understand the significance.

"So?" Donna tried to think how she'd feel about being forced to review an old lover's restaurant as part of her job. Would she give it a glowing review out of respect for what they shared or would she rip into him for how he abandoned her? "Does it say how they broke up?"

"No, but she hoped to rekindle the relationship by writing a spectacular review for him. Once the review was printed, then Sylvester, or I should say, George, could grab the executive chef job at an exclusive Bahamas resort. He'd even contacted Jane to be his reference. Whatever he told her made her think they could rekindle the fire. She even wrote he was the love of her life. She couldn't wait to leave behind her critic job and stroll along the beach with him."

It all sounded good in theory, but that meant the other players had to play along. "How would the paper react to the review, especially since it wasn't the one they wanted?"

"The woman had worked it out. She would rip into the other three restaurants, and she had a big exposé about Norelle's."

Maria clapped her hands together. "It has to be about their Wall of Death, right?"

Cecilia shook her head, slowly prolonging their wait.

"Come on, Daniel will be here in five minutes to make sure Maria is safe since she wasn't home on time."

Her mother shot a guilty look at her daughter-in-law. "Sorry, I don't mean to cause any undue tension."

She waved the worry aside. "No problem. He's just a bit overprotective. It's cute in a way. Please go on with the story."

"Norelle's used to be called Cajun Quarters down in New Orleans. While it was a popular restaurant, Jane's review had mentioned they used past-dated meat and seafood. That type of stuff made people sick. A dozen or more people tried to sue, but the restaurant went out of business and declared bankruptcy. They probably thought North Carolina was far enough away from New Orleans that no one would know them. There must be a gossip hotline about the visit because she received a threatening phone call, telling her it would be smarter not to come."

When it came to clues, how much clearer could it be? "Who called?"

Cecilia's finger traced the lines of script. "It doesn't say."

Maria rubbed her eyes. "I'm too tired to figure this out. You know it wasn't George."

"Why?" Donna figured whoever owned Norelle's could also be guilty of foul play. Still, she wouldn't discount anyone, not even Janice, who knew J.E. was coming and possibly her intentions to slam The Croaking Frog.

"I think," Maria glanced at both women, "George/Sylvester was trying to sweeten her up, playing on their previous relationship for a good review. Word around town is the man considers himself a player, despite living with Linona Faber for the last five years."

"That's right." Her mother leaned forward and spoke in a rush. "Linona owns that whole strip mall, from the restaurant to the antique shop. When they first set up house, people thought he was using her, but since they've been together five years, they're practically married now."

Maria held up a hand as if awaiting a turn. "Jane, J.E, would have recognized his voice."

A knock on the bedroom door silenced the three of them. Donna eased off the bed and flipped off the overhead light. Would a killer knock? He would if he wanted to fool them.

Chapter Nine

DONNA HELD HER breath, hoping whoever it was would quietly walk away. There'd be no reason for any of the guests to bang on another guest's door. Since she thought it more important to preserve the house's Victorian charm as much as possible, she hadn't installed peepholes. Besides, even if it was sixty dollars a door times eight, it was almost five hundred dollars. She should have bit the financial bullet. It would at least allow her to see the face of her killer.

The door trembled underneath another knock. "I know you're in there! When Maria didn't come home on time, I tried calling. Even Mark Taber called me and asked me why Donna wasn't answering her phone."

It was Daniel. Her pent-up breath came out in a whoosh.

"Then I called Donna. No answer."

She flipped the lights back on and had her hand on the door to open it as her brother kept talking.

"I even called Mother and no answer. Then a horrible thought occurred to me. What catastrophic event might happen if the three of you got together?"

Donna removed her hand from the knob and patted her pockets for her phone. She pulled it out and noticed it was on silent. She had probably muted it when tailing J.E. There were also several calls from Mark and a text. DO NOT GO INTO J.E.'S ROOM. There was no reason for the man to yell about it. Then again, he wasn't a good texter and could have been in a hurry. What he really meant was don't go in the room and mess it up. She signaled to her mother and Maria to put everything back.

Her mother snapped the suitcase shut while Maria smoothed the bedspread.

Donna swung open the door. "Daniel, what a surprise to see you here."

"Yeah, and I suppose the three of you weren't snooping."

She decided it was a rhetorical question. "I better check on my cinnamon roll dough." She bumped her brother the tiniest bit as she pushed past him.

Her mother followed close behind. Kissing her son's cheek before murmuring, "You know I never turn on my cell phone when I'm driving. I don't want to be distracted."

Donna was too far away to hear Maria's excuse. Out of the three of them, she'd have the best chance of wiggling her way out. Who did her brother think he was anyhow? His behavior reminded her of their father's. It made her question if she was more like her mother.

Cecilia entered the kitchen and pawed through her purse. "Here it is." She held up her mobile, attired in a leopard skin case. "Oh, I missed Jason's call."

It was nice her mother had a gentleman companion. She needed someone to watch television with and to challenge her on crossword puzzles.

"Tim called too, and Omar."

Donna did a double take and then punched down the dough sitting in a metal bowl. Did she know this woman? "Are you calling them back?"

"No. A woman has to make a man work for it."

Work for what? She didn't want to know. Her thumbs sunk into the dough. The rolls would rise again overnight after she shaped them. Donna turned the oven on just enough to warm itself. Then she'd switch it off, providing enough residual heat for the rolls to rise, but not bake.

Her mother shouldered her purse and pulled out her car keys. She moved around the stove and craned her neck to look Donna in the eye. "You'd do well to follow my example. Make up a profile. Go out on dates. I bet that would bring your detective to your door more often."

Donna managed a strained smile, unwilling to admit inconvenient murders kept the man around most of the time. "I'll think about it."

Cecilia wrapped her arms around Donna in a half embrace and kissed her cheek. "Remember, I care about you. Don't overlook widowers or single fathers. I still plan on being a grandmother."

The kitchen door that was partially open had now swung shut. Her brother and Maria would take the side entrance to avoid any inquiries on the grandbaby front. *Cowards.*

"You still have Jasper."

Her mother sniffed. "I prefer a grandson who doesn't pee on my peonies. They had no color this year, all washed out. I blame that on Jasper."

"Bye now. Drive safe." She hoped her mother would take the hint. She had no way to defend Jasper since he tended to pee on anything bigger than him. Almost the entire world was bigger than he was. It was a plus he kept his watering efforts outside.

Donna locked the front door after her mother left and then moved to the side door to lock it also when a face appeared on the other side. Her heart turned over as a cold chill drew the hairs on her neck to an upright position. She blinked, her fingers frozen on the deadbolt.

"Donna, it's me."

Her shoulders relaxed. Even thought it was hard to make out features on the unlit porch, she recognized Mark's voice. *Thank goodness.* She didn't know if she had enough energy to battle a would-be murderer with the day she'd had. Her hand twisted the knob and pulled the door back. "Come for your dog?"

"Not really, I thought you could keep her."

This is how it started, forgetting to pick up the dog. "I only have one dog bed, and it's already spoken for. Not even sure it would fit Loralee."

"Ah, Donna." His hand rubbed over his face and continued through his thick salt-and-pepper hair. "It's been a day and a half. I'm not up to dealing with dogs right now. Maybe tomorrow. I only came by because you weren't answering your phone."

"It was on silent. Daniel pointed it out to me after you called him." She arched her brows and cocked her head. "It made me feel like I was seven years old."

"Sorry. I was worried."

He did care about her. Mother had no clue what she was talking about.

Mark paused to scratch his head but continued speaking. "You mess around in J.E.'s room tonight? You know what I mean."

She did know. Her hand went to her neck, tugged at her neckline. Maybe she should have left the rolls out since it felt plenty warm. "Did you mean did I clean the room? Yes, I did, but at the time, no one knew anything specific. I noticed she's a tidy traveler."

"Traveler no more. The woman has hit the end of her journey." Mark delivered the abrupt summation in a weary voice. He didn't know J.E. had plans to restart her life. "They found her body not too far from the car."

Anticipating the news, she wasn't shocked. "How did she die?" It probably wasn't by natural means. The woman wasn't old enough to die from old age. Her sexy nightie and plans to live in the Caribbean suggested robust health.

"Good question. It is presumed to be suicide at this point." He gestured in the direction of the kitchen. Donna locked the side door to prevent any more visitors and followed him.

"Have you eaten?" She knew he hadn't. Mark would immerse himself in a case so deep, if breathing weren't an involuntary response, he'd suffocate. His hopeful expression had her opening the fridge and pulling out some leftover ham and cheese rolls and lasagna roll-ups.

The man practically levitated off his seat at the sight of food. She placed the tidbits in the toaster oven since the microwave would make them soggy. "Makes me wonder if you came to see about my safety or the possibility of a snack."

"I wouldn't even have knocked, but I saw your brother in the parking lot, and he told me you were expecting me."

"That's odd. Not that you saw Daniel but that he thought I was expecting you. Maybe he thought you came to pick up your dog." She flung her hand out to the side of the kitchen were Loralee and Jasper were curled into a dog circle sleeping. Neither one of them had bothered to bark. "Your dog is a bad influence on my dog."

"Loralee is not a bad influence. Perhaps Jasper needed some calming down. He's mellowed under the influence of a mature female."

Donna narrowed her eyes in case he was comparing her to Loralee. "How do you know it is J.E.? It could be someone impersonating her since no one truly knows if J.E. is a man or a woman."

"Honestly, where do you come up with these ideas?"

It was probable. It always served as a plot device in mystery movies and books. "Maria thought of it, but still, it could happen." A twinge spasmed across her shoulders due to blaming her sister-in-law. When it came to guilt, she could create an entire ensemble from it.

"Not in Legacy. People die from strokes, heart attacks, car wrecks, and on occasion, a domestic altercation. There is no record of someone pretending to be someone else dying or committing suicide in Legacy. I know. I've been on the force thirty-three years."

The man wasn't going to budge on this, which was sad because she would have liked J.E. to have made it to a tropical island to start a new life, even if it was with a slimy character like George. Should she call him Sylvester to keep things straight? "Why would a well-known critic come to Legacy to kill herself?"

"That part puzzles me. That's another reason I'm here. If anyone could sniff out a motive or toss a room, it would be you." He wiggled his eyebrows, surprising a laugh out of her when she wanted to be mad about his assumption.

The scent of ham and the underlying smell of garlic had her checking the toaster oven. "You really need some vegetables." She donned an oven glove before sliding the hot tray out and moving the food onto a plate that she carried to the counter by the fridge instead of to Mark.

"Hey! Where are you going with my food?"

Donna ignored his inquiry as she picked out a cucumber slice, one baby Bella mushroom, and a small parsnip. She arranged them on top of a spinach leaf. "It's not much, but if you eat them, I might be able to find you some cheesecake."

He held out his hands for the plate. "As hungry as I am, you'll be lucky if I don't eat the plate, so you might as well start looking for the cheesecake."

Donna wrinkled her nose as she handed him the plate. A quick freezer search netted an individually wrapped slice. She'd never admit to baking a cheesecake and wrapping individual slices just in case he dropped by. That would stay her secret. She also wouldn't confess to knowing she could get the man to jump through hoops with the promise of food. The foil-wrapped cheesecake went into the still warm toaster oven to take the chill off it. A tall glass of milk joined the nibbles.

He grimaced. "Milk?"

"Yes. The last thing you need this time of night is coffee. Let me get you a fork." She handed him the utensil and napkin and drew another stool to the island.

"Do you want to know what I found or do you prefer not to know?" A pleased smile tugged her lips upward, because frankly, she enjoyed being one step ahead of the police despite all the claims about civilians contaminating the area.

"I'm here." He cut the lasagna roll-up with the fork and shoved it in his mouth.

"You could have come for the food."

He snorted his response through a closed mouth, but she got the gist of it.

"J.E. kept a journal of sorts, writing down her plans. The woman had some primo plans to quit being a critic and move to the Bahamas. She even expected Sylvester from Sylvester's Salon to go with her. They knew each other from chef school back when Sylvester was known as George. J.E. was going to write this glowing review to help him get the executive chef job at a Bahamian Resort. In her journal, she thinks he's crazy about her. Maria thinks the man had J.E. buffaloed because he's living with Linona Faber."

Mark took a swig of milk and swallowed. "You got all of this from a date book?"

Her fingers wrapped around a salt shaker and walked it across the table, making it take sharp turns as if marching. "We got much, *much* more."

"We?" His cheeks rounded, rather like a cherub, as he blew out a long breath. "Who is we? I hope all your guests weren't sitting around for a read aloud from the journal."

Donna stopped playing with the salt shaker. She slapped both hands against the island top and pushed to stand. She opened the toaster oven to check on the cheesecake. Cool, but not frozen, and easy enough to unwrap at this stage. The swirl of caramel pleased her. The great thing about cooking was if you followed the directions, things turned out the way they should. Too bad the same principles never applied to life.

She carried the plate over and placed it in front of Mark. Despite her delay in replying, the man said nothing. Just her luck that he played the silent game better than she did. "It was only me, Maria, and my mother."

"Your mother! Why not invite your second cousin, once removed?"

"If you knew Doris, you'd understand why no one invites her to anything. My mother was here, which is a good thing since the journal is written in shorthand. She's the only one who could read it. Can you read shorthand?"

"No, but there's bound to be someone who can. How do you know she wasn't making it up?"

Donna took a step back. "Are you kidding me? I'm not sure you and I can be friends if you'd accuse my mother of pretending to read a dead woman's diary for some desperate need for attention. You've never met my mother."

"Ha. I imagine you get your feistiness from her. It's my job to be skeptical. Why do you think she wasn't making it up?"

It was her turn to show him how wrong he was. "J.E.'s sense of taste was damaged due to radiation treatments she had for cancer. She knew she couldn't be an effective critic. The last review she wrote was pleasant in comparison to previous ones since she couldn't taste the food."

"Sounds like a good reason for suicide to me."

She crossed her arms and tapped her toe. Why wasn't the man getting it? "The newspaper sent her down here with orders to rip into the restaurants. Bad reviews sell newspapers. The more virulent the review the more people read it. They didn't care about the chefs or employees that would lose their income. They just wanted blood, the ink kind."

"Okay, you're telling me at this point J.E. isn't really writing the reviews, but is more following directions on how to write the reviews?"

"Yes." Her arms fell to her side. Perhaps he did understand. She shoved one hip up on the stool, then wiggled into a stable position.

"How could she write her boyfriend a glowing review?" Mark pushed his empty plate away and reached for the cheesecake.

"I wondered that myself. It could be she brokered a deal of sorts. One glowing review for a tell-all expose. Norelle's has a past that J.E. knew about. It wasn't pretty. It involved lawsuits, bankruptcy, and tainted food."

"The tainted food could explain the Wall of Death."

He placed a bite of cheesecake in his mouth and closed his eyes reverently. You have to respect a man who gave food the proper adoration it deserved. What might appear to be cream cheese, eggs, butter, vanilla, and sugar mixed up in a tasty dessert was much, much more. Mark understood this. Each recipe she made was an extension of herself. No wonder chefs got so worked up about bad reviews.

"I don't know. I do know J.E. got a threatening phone call telling her not to come to Legacy," Donna told him.

"Man or woman?"

"She didn't write down whether she knew if it was a man or a woman."

"It could have been your friend, Janice."

First, he accused her mother of making up stuff, now Janice was a killer. "Janice is no murderer."

"Peace." He held up both hands, palms facing out. "Let me preface this by saying I don't think Janice is a killer. Still…" He held up one finger, quelling whatever thought Donna wanted to add. "Whenever some horrible crime has been committed, you get the neighbors on television who talk about what a quiet man the fellow was or how he helped roll out the elderly lady's trash."

"Those people were not observant. I would know." She'd seen enough of the people smiling at the camera while discussing a grizzly murder. "Good chance they never ran the ones that suspected something was up. Probably didn't play as well."

There were times when Janice could be an emotional rollercoaster when it came to her restaurant. Donna considered herself driven when it came to the inn, but she was an amateur compared to Janice. "What if Janice did call J.E. and disguised her voice? The journal didn't mention a death threat, just a warning not to come."

"All the attention is on the person who showed the bad judgment to call and threaten J.E." She brandished her closed right fist. "In the meantime, if there is a murderer, then he or she blends into the background." She placed her left hand behind her back.

"Show me what you have in your left hand?"

Donna brought her fist back up to the island top, opened it, revealing the salt shaker.

"I never saw you take it, which shows how tired I am. You have a legitimate point, although I know you're fighting for your friend who is guilty of poor judgment. If J.E. was still alive, she could press terroristic threatening charges. Of course, that would depend on knowing who made the call. We don't."

"Where did you find her?" He'd probably refuse to tell her, citing it was police business.

"Ha! Probably think you'll trick me into telling you." He shook his head. "It will be in the paper soon enough. That nephew of mine must sit by the police scanner." His hand wrapped around his neck and rubbed it. Mark yawned, blinked twice, then forced his eyes wide before letting them droop to half open. "You already know most of it. A citizen called about an empty white car running near the edge of the town limits. An officer showed up. By that time the car had run out of gas, and he found a woman in the woods about ten yards from the car. Face down, her arms flung out, and her cell phone about a yard away as if it bounced out of her hand."

Donna rubbed a knuckle between her eyes and yawned. "Why was it labeled suicide if it looked like she was running?"

"The paramedic mentioned blue lips and skin as a sign of poisoning. Everyone knows women tend to overdose on drugs as opposed to shooting themselves."

She covered her second yawn with her hand. She needed sleep, especially since her guests would be expecting a five-star breakfast. Too bad she hadn't pawned Loralee off on her mother. "There's a big difference between poison and drugs. I would assume women resort to drugs because they don't want to feel pain or be messy. Poison is painful and messy. It can result in everything from nausea to hallucinations and everything in between from breathing issues to diarrhea. Does that sound like something someone would want to experience? Poison used to be the murder tool of women in the Renaissance period. Women would conceal it in their rings and poison their enemies and unfaithful lovers or husbands."

"Whoa, maybe I should think twice about the free food." He tried to grin to negate the remark.

"You know I'm a nurse. I've seen more than one accidental poisoning, although a few may have been on purpose. If discovered in time, people can be saved. Here's an ironic twist. How would you kill a food critic?"

"Put it in her food or drink." He folded his hands and rested his chin on top of them. "I seriously hope I can remember this tomorrow. We'll come by with an official information recovery search and pick up the notebook then. Anything else?"

She held up two fingers. "There was a sticky note with the names of restaurants I think she was going to review. She had Sylvester's crossed off."

"Interesting. Who else was on the list?"

"Norelle's, The Croaking Frog, and Culinary Cousins."

"Hmm, never heard of Culinary Cousins."

"Janice told me it's some South Carolina eatery fronted by two former cheerleaders."

"Janice?" The brushy eyebrows lifted.

Ah, she knew what he was asking. Instead of answering how

many people she'd discussed the note with, Donna distracted with more info. "When I was getting ready for the mixer, the land line rang. It was a man trying to reach J.E. When I asked if he'd like to leave a message, he hung up. By that time, J.E. would have been dead, but whoever called didn't know she was dead or why would he call?"

Mark's eyes closed, making her think he was asleep, but he still managed a response. "Could be the killer wasn't that experienced in the use of poison. J.E. was driving somewhere. So wherever she ingested it, she had enough strength to drive. She also had the cell phone in her hand. We're running a search on everyone she called. Her sister should be in tomorrow to identify the body."

"Go home. You're barely awake. Let me put the dishes away, and I'll follow you home."

Mark opened his eyes and managed a dopey smile. "That's the best offer I've had in years."

"Don't get too excited. I just want to make sure you make it home alive so you can provide Loralee with a good home."

His body jerked, resembling someone who'd stuck a fork in an outlet. "I don't have any pet supplies."

Donna placed the dishes in the dishwasher and turned it on while she talked. "I know. You really need to think about getting some. If you don't take the dog, I may have to work on my mother. The woman is gone every night of the week. Loralee would be better off with you."

Mark bent over and shook Loralee and Jasper awake. "Let's go fellows." The dogs pushed up, swayed a bit, and followed the detective to the backyard. Donna locked up, thankful she had Tennyson to start the coffee and put the hot water and tea fixings out. People could wait as long as they had coffee and the promise of breakfast.

Mark and the dogs waited beside the steps. "Why is your mother busy every night? Isn't she a widow?"

"That's the reason. She has men standing in line to wine and dine her. When I asked for some children's movies, she brought them and some profiles of men who'd contacted her that she thought would be perfect for me."

Mark grumbled. It pleased her that he was annoyed at her mother's matchmaking. She couldn't resist the tiniest poke. After all, the man shouldn't take her for granted. "I wasn't interested in any of her wealthy, retired men who wanted to travel the world with the right companion."

"Sensible."

"No, too old, but she's been getting flirts from younger men." She left it at that as she herded the dogs into the car. Donna would have laughed at Mark's befuddled expression but it would have been rude, and she didn't have the energy.

Chapter Ten

THE SCENT OF brewing coffee not only tantalized Donna's nose, but allowed her to heave a satisfied sigh. At last, Tennyson was earning his keep. There were times she despaired of teaching the college student the most general chores. He sometimes acted as if he'd arrived from another planet, a place where they never did common chores such as cooking or cleaning or doing the laundry. To be fair, she couldn't say he wasn't willing, only that he needed constant supervision.

Her entrance through the front door allowed her to see how guests might see The Painted Lady Inn. Realistically, the guests probably breezed in never noticing that the wall art picked out the colors in the floral runner. The coffee perked in its conference-size pot, while a plate of biscotti and a carafe of hot water with a nearby basket of tea bags waited for sleepy guests to arrive. Sugar, creamer, cut lemons, honey, everything was there. This was an absolute first. Her lips tipped up. Finally, she could congratulate Tennyson on a job well done.

Her hand was on the kitchen door when she heard voices. There shouldn't be anyone else in the kitchen unless Tennyson had started talking to himself and was able to imitate a woman's voice.

"I don't mind helping you set up the coffee. I better head back home before Uncle Herman wakes."

Ah, Winnie. No wonder everything was spot on. Maybe she

should try to get Winnie to take over Tennyson's job.

"Thanks. I really appreciate your help and couldn't have done it without you. You're the best."

Donna cringed on the other side of the door listening to her helper pile on the gratitude. *Please, have some pride.* The back door slammed in the distance, indicating Winnie had left. Donna waited a few seconds longer, not wanting Tennyson to think she'd eavesdropped on the conversation, although it would be interesting to hear what lie he might concoct about the work being done.

"Good morning." She breezed into the kitchen as if that were her original purpose as opposed to lingering by the door. "The dining room looks great. Well done. I may make an innkeeper out of you yet."

Tennyson laughed, flushed, and then smiled. "I asked Winnie to come over and help me. I probably could have done it on my own, but females love to help."

Did women love to help? Better yet, was helping a ploy that men used to attract women? Her eyes narrowed as she analyzed the gangling young man in front of her, with his barely-there beard stubble and shaggy hair. No one would accuse him of being a player or someone with enough experience to know that girls liked to help. "You heard the front door bell jingle."

"I did." He shuffled his feet as he pushed his hands into his pockets. "I could have set everything up on my own."

"You'll have plenty of time to do that. Winnie's only staying for a week." Donna opened the oven door to pull out the rolls she left to rise. They were rounded and plump as she expected.

"I know."

The desolation in Tennyson's voice tugged at her heartstrings, but she had no experience with lovestruck boys, or girls for that matter. Whenever a nurse arrived red-eyed and weary after an emotional breakup, Donna told them they were better off without the albatross around their neck. Most missed the literary reference and broke into tears again. One had the temerity to label her *Heartless Tollhouse*. There would have to be some way she could bolster Tennyson's spirits before he became even moodier, due to Winnie's impending departure.

"You have a car. Winnie lives within driving distance." The possibility that the thwarted Romeo might become a stalker forced her to tack on, "If things work out between the two of you."

"I do have a car." His shoulders went back and his chin lifted. Just like that, all was right with the world. "Where are the dogs?"

"I left them with my mother. Today may be a crazy day." No need to add she expected the police to arrive and search J.E.'s room. Maybe her sister would swing by and get her stuff. It would be nice if they could be a little low key about it. No flashing lights or parking the squad car in the parking lot entrance blocking everyone. It would be even better if they showed up after everyone took off for their adventures.

The brochure holder she placed on the Pembroke table had attractions for the tri-county area. If they actually took the brochure with them and showed the merchant, the guest and Donna both got a little something. An extra bottle of wine from a winery she had appreciated. However, she refused to place the wood cutout of grandma bending over showing her bloomers anywhere on the premises.

Tennyson got started on the juice and ice water as she warmed the sour cream chicken quiche in the toaster oven. The rolls went back into the convection oven, then it would be time to start on the bacon. She wanted to try the breakfast pizza, but it wasn't something she could make ahead, like the quiche. "Ten?" She only resorted to his shortened name when in a hurry. "Can you go into the cellar freezer and get me the soy patties?"

"Will do." He clomped off without a fuss. Usually, he went on about special diets and meat preferences being an effort to gain more attention or emotional control over your life by refusing to consume certain foods.

It didn't matter to Donna why a guest did or didn't want something. She'd give them whatever they wanted if possible and profitable, although there was no reason to go crazy about it and insist on a separate kitchen and dishes. Maria did put a disclaimer on the website that tree nuts, as opposed to the people nuts, were used in the kitchen. Sometimes the people nuts just worked in the kitchen.

The back door slammed, causing Donna to suck in her lips. *Please don't be the police. Wait, they'd use the front door.* A quick peek over a shoulder revealed Maria. "What are you doing here? You're supposed to have the day off."

"I know." Maria stowed her purse and reached for an apron. "I started the laundry. Daniel took off to examine some building site problem before the load had finished. That put an immediate halt to our day together. I figured I'd help you with breakfast and maybe my husband might be home by then. I'm not holding my breath since any problem that occurs on the weekend usually ends up swallowing both Saturday and Sunday."

"I can use the help. Could you whip up the batter for the vegan crepes?"

Maria flipped open the recipe book to a folded page and assembled the ingredients on the island. "You remember what happened last time you made a vegan option?"

Donna rolled her eyes. "Everyone else wanted it since they felt like they were being cheated out of something. Maybe they'll come down last this morning. Anyhow, they can't be too picky if they're staying here."

"We're not exactly California. If they want a vegetarian restaurant, they'd have to drive. I need to crunch the numbers to see if offering vegan meals is profitable."

"Don't bother." She rolled her shoulders as she stood at the stove. Her joints ached from lack of sleep, and being on her feet for almost twenty hours didn't help. For some insane reason, she thought running a B and B to be less work than nursing. "As for it being profitable, not hardly. No one wants those tofu patties. I can't even get Jasper to eat them. All the same, I can't tell people I can't serve them breakfast because of their food choices. It's a B and B, not a B."

"Yeah, you have a point."

Tennyson brought the much-talked-about soy sausages and placed them on the counter. He started to walk away.

"Wait just a minute, Tennyson. It's time to bring you into the cooking club."

"I'm not ready."

A whine colored his reply. It made him sound even more immature, but she wouldn't mention it because he'd turn petulant and pout the rest of the day.

"Put them in the microwave on defrost for two minutes."

Out of the corner of her eye, Donna saw the entire soy link box go into the microwave. "Not the entire box, the plastic will melt onto the links."

Tennyson shot her an offended look.

Maria laughed, but stopped abruptly when both Tennyson and

Donna glared at her.

Her inexperienced helper gestured to the microwave. "You never mentioned opening the box and taking the links out of the plastic."

Donna took a deep breath and closed her eyes. Even Daniel had left home with basic cooking skills. It didn't seem possible a person could grow up and not know how to defrost something. "True." She turned to Tennyson, pushing out words she almost never said. "It's my fault. Take the links out of the package. Place them on a microwavable plate with a paper towel over it, then put them in the microwave."

Tennyson followed her direction, his actions slow and deliberate as if he'd never done it before. It made Donna wonder if anyone cooked at his home. "What did you have for breakfast growing up?"

"Cereal. On the weekends, we had donuts."

No wonder Tennyson resembled a walking scarecrow. It also explained why he ate whatever she gave him without complaint. Mark's sudden appearance in the kitchen interrupted her delving into Tennyson's childhood eating patterns. A uniformed officer stood beside Mark.

The man looked apologetic, she'd give him that much, but now was absolutely the worst time.

"Morning Donna, Maria, Tennyson."

She knew why he was here. The fact he came in the unlocked back door was a plus. "You didn't leave the lights on your car flashing, did you?" She directed the question to the young officer. Where was Officer Wells? At least she knew him. This new officer appeared to be about as old as Tennyson and just as thin.

"No, ma'am."

"Good. Now's not a good time. It's breakfast. Why don't the two of you sit down at the counter, and I'll serve you a hearty breakfast, then once everyone leaves the dining room you can dig through the bedroom as much as you please."

The patrolman blinked, then cut his eyes to Mark, expecting the higher-ranked person to make the decision.

"Sounds doable. I'll go grab us a couple cups of coffee." Mark suited his actions to his words, going to the dining room.

No one would comment on Mark, thinking he was one of the guests. He dropped in so much the neighbors must assume he was part owner, investigating a crime, or that he was carrying on a torrid affair with the actual owner. Too bad that a possible crime served as the real reason.

Mark came back in with the cups. "There's three in the dining room."

"It's not the vegans, is it?" Maria stirred while talking. "I'm not ready for them."

"Ah." Mark handed his fellow officer his cup and placed his own on the counter top. His hand cupped his chin, rubbing the leftover stubble. "It's a middle-aged couple with their teenage son. Look to me like the meat and potatoes type."

"The Thompsons. I'll start them with cinnamon rolls." She pulled the oversized rolls out of the oven and onto the cooling rack.

"I wouldn't mind a cinnamon roll to start with." Mark winked at her.

The wink always confused her. She had an uncle who would always tell a whopper of a lie, and then he winked. It was always a secret signal between the two of them that he was lying. At the time, she thought no one knew it but her. Later on, she realized everyone did.

She iced the hot rolls and plated them. "Tennyson. Go take these rolls out."

His fingers splayed across his chest. "Me? You want me to take them out?"

When she first hired Tennyson she tried to keep him totally behind the scenes, afraid he might do or say something awkward. It became apparent there was only so much to do behind the scenes. "Yes. You. Say good morning. Ask if they have any plans for the day. You did a wonderful job with Scarlett. Be yourself." Donna winced on the last statement. Truthfully, she had no clue who the real Tennyson was. The philosophy-spouting version was probably the college edition. Once he changed majors, his behavior would probably alter, too.

The front bell jingled as Tennyson left the room beaming as if Donna had given him a hundred-dollar bill. "Who can that be?" Donna plated the quiche while Maria added three strips of bacon to the plates. Mark stood up. "I'll check."

The young officer stopped eating and shot a look at the door, probably debating if he should unholster his gun and follow.

Mark returned before things got interesting. "Some woman wants to know about a book group club or something. She's really aggressive. Telling me what she wants served and what all. It's supposed to be tonight, I think."

Why did she want to be in their stupid group, anyhow? It was obvious they were getting her to cook and use her place free of charge when there had been no attempt to invite her in time to read the book. No one had even told her what the book was about.

Maria placed her hand on her shoulder. "I'll talk to her. I know how to handle aggressive people."

Sweat beaded Donna's face as she took deep breaths, trying to slow her breathing, She held up one hand. "I know you can handle aggressive people, because you do such a good job with me." She pointed her thumb back to herself. "I'll handle this one, bless her heart. You deliver the quiches."

The young officer swiveled his head between the two, unsure if he was in the midst of a domestic altercation. Mark put down the roll long enough to address his colleague's agitation. "We stay in the kitchen."

Donna wiped her hands on her apron and went into the foyer where she spotted no one. A quick peek in the dining room didn't reveal any neighbors. In the wedding parlor, she found the artificial woman she'd encountered the day before. She was lounging on the Victorian chaise with her shoes on the white velvet. Who did that? How would she like it if Donna marched into her house and put her dirty shoes on her couch? She struggled for a name and came up empty.

"Mark tells me you're here about the book group."

The woman held out a piece of paper, never even bothering to get up off the lounge. Donna stepped forward to take the paper, wondering how she could knock her feet off the velvet.

The paper included a list of seven extravagant appetizers including lobster rolls, asparagus wrapped in prosciutto, and roasted Moroccan spiced salmon. Whatever happened to cookies and coffee? The book club must have thought she would pay dearly to rub elbows with the stiff-backed matrons and Botox-filled second wives.

"This is a nice menu. It might work out well for future functions."

The woman lowered her chin. "It's for the book club. Tomorrow."

Donna could have sworn the invitation listed a different night, but this was who they were, people who had no respect for other people's time or money.

"There's a conflict. I can't do it. I must have misheard the date."

If she was upset, startled, or even confused, it was hard to tell because her face didn't move. "Monday?"

"Busy."

"You can't be. The inn isn't open on Monday." The woman sat up finally, swinging her feet to the floor. She could have felt at a disadvantage at her lower height.

It was like that. She was supposed to jump through some hoop. The large mirror over the mantle reflected her red face back to her, complete with furrowed brows and balled hands on her hips. Donna didn't like the fact she looked like a fishwife ready to wade into a fight. Her hands dropped to her side as she relaxed her face. *Remember, you're just as good as anyone of them.*

"How kind of you to notice. All the same, I'm much too busy to be a *part* of your book club."

The book club envoy stood slowly. "Tuesday?"

There must have been a horrible mishap in the woman's liposuction that had sucked out brain cells, too. "No-day. There is *no* day I want to have the book club at my inn."

The woman pivoted on her platform shoes and headed for the door with her nose up high enough she might run into something. If everyone in the book club had the same attitude, they might show up anyway, expecting her to trot out treats, thinking it was a fait accompli by their mere presence.

Donna caught up with the woman at the door. "Don't bother showing up with your book-toting friends, thinking I'll invite you in. That's not how things work around here, girlfriend."

The woman gasped and grabbed the door with the obvious intention of slamming it. Donna held onto it, not wanting any anger taken out on her etched-glass panels. The woman tugged on the door, but Donna held firm.

Finally, the woman released her grip and hissed. "You'll never be invited again."

Donna knew the woman was probably speaking the truth. "That's a chance I'll have to take." She closed the door gently and made a sharp turn only to see Maria, Tennyson, and Mark peeking out of the kitchen door.

Back in the kitchen, she created the plates for the vegans, who were considerate enough to come down last.

The patrolman Mark introduced as Cody raved about the quiche. "I never ate quiche before, thinking it was a girly food. Detective Taber was right. He said if we got here early enough, we'd get served an excellent breakfast free of charge."

"Oh, really?" She pretended shock, but she knew better. "Once I get the final couple served, I'll close the dining room door and Maria can open the bedroom for you."

With any luck, nothing had changed from their previous search. When it came to criminal matters, luck never served her.

Chapter Eleven

THE DISHWASHER CHUGGED softly as Donna used a scouring pad to attack the cookie sheet waiting in the industrial sink. A commercial dishwasher would be nice, but she couldn't justify the expense with, at the most, twenty people sitting down to breakfast. A conveyor belt Hobart wasn't in her future. If she had thousands to throw away, she'd spend it on some type of lift. An elevator would guarantee a more senior clientele. Donna wrinkled her nose and considered the inn filled with women similar to her former guest, Eunice Ledbetter. The lively crone not only attempted to talk her way out of paying for room and board, but also had a felonious streak.

"Nope. Don't need that."

Mark slipped up behind her. "Don't need what?"

Donna dropped the cookie sheet with a clunk. She closed her eyes, thankful she hadn't shrieked. The man would never let her hear the end of it. "What do you want?" Her tone may have been more abrupt than she wished, but it covered her unexpected moment of fright.

"You mentioned a notebook in the suitcase. No notebook. Some interesting clothing choices, expensive shoes, and probably ten pounds of toiletries, but no book."

What could have happened to the book? Donna dried her rubber glove clad hands, then tugged the fingers free one finger at a time. "I'll go look for it. Sometimes men fail to move things around."

"Move things around." Mark's face twitched as if suppressing an expression. "Would that be an expert amateur sleuth expression?"

When the man got like this it was hard to decide if he were teasing her or baiting her. She balled her hands on her hips. "It's neither. It's simply the truth. Everyone knows men tend to look in a room, cabinet, garage, and give the place a casual survey, then announce that the item can't be found."

"So that's what you think of men?" Mark reached into his sports coat and pulled out his ever-present notebook. He flipped a few pages until he came to an itemized list and held it out for Donna's perusal.

"What's this?" The list included two pairs of leggings, khaki trousers, and a paperback entitled *Romancing the Chef*. Donna would have liked to see the book to decide if it was fiction or nonfiction. The list went on in detail for forty-eight more items including earrings and earring backs.

"It's everything in J.E.'s suitcase. We took photos too." He hoisted a bushy eyebrow. "Do you think we still need to look around?"

She continued to stare at the list. "I never saw the food thermometer or the chakra crystal set. You're certainly thorough, but where is the notebook?"

"Ah, that was my question."

"I know." She held up her hand. "Let me think about this. We locked the door last night so no one would *accidentally* go into the room. It wasn't unlocked until just now." Her eyes flickered upward as she tried to remember the room last night. There were no open windows. Besides, a person would have to know about the notebook to snatch it. Better yet, they'd have to know what was actually written on the pages. As far as she knew, the only person who fit that description was... "Mother!" Her eyes cut to Mark hoping he didn't catch her verbal slip. In an inspired moment she added, "of all things holy."

Her hand dropped when she realized her own parent compromised evidence. Perhaps she could get the book back without revealing who took it. A phone call should do it, but she needed to get rid of Mark first. "Go look in the bathroom. It's really quite spacious."

He crossed his arms and leaned against the island. "I will after you call your mother."

Her hand went to her throat and stroked it. *Save me from intelligent detectives.* Her right hand slipped into her apron pocket and retrieved her phone. "I could use some privacy."

Mark shook his head and had the nerve to grin. "I want to hear this. Could be the apple didn't fall too far from the tree."

Her thumb depressed the four, speed dialing her mother. She actually hoped her mother took the book because if she didn't, it meant someone had entered the inn and stole it, not a thought she welcomed. The phone rang and rang. She glanced at Mark, who appeared unconcerned. Too bad she didn't have his confidence. By the fifth ring, she was wondering why her mother didn't have voice mail. The only reason she held the phone up to her ear for so long was she didn't have any clever remarks to send Mark back to searching the room. The only good clue may have gone home with her parent. By the seventh ring, a breathless Cecilia answered.

"Goodness, you don't give up. I was busy."

"Doing what?" As soon as the words were out of her mouth, she regretted them. With her mother's dive into the dating pool, she might not want to know what made her mother so breathless. "No, never mind, I don't want to know."

"Oh yes, you do." Her mother teased in a singsong voice. "You're going to like what I did."

Donna scowled. How could she stop her mother? Worse yet, Mark was leaning in closer. She could have sworn he was at the end of the island when she started the conversation and now he was in the middle. The man must have inched closer to hear better. She turned her back and cupped her free hand around the phone to make it harder for the eavesdropper. Somehow, her sudden move depressed the speaker key. Her mother's cheery voice filled the kitchen.

"I translated the entire notebook into a typed transcript."

"You weren't supposed to take the notebook. Capiche?" She realized the phone was still on speaker and punched at the key. Mark lifted the phone from her.

"Detective Mark Taber here. I assume I'm talking to Mrs. Tollhouse."

She couldn't hear what her mother said, but it caused Mark to cut his eyes in her direction. "She said what?"

Could her mother be bold enough to mention their conversation from the night before?

"That's very nice of you...I appreciate your hard work, but the notebook is evidence... Yes, I'd love to have it back....Yeah, I'll be here." He handed the phone back to her. "She's bringing it by, along with the transcript. After talking to your mother, I understand you much, much better."

Donna opened her mouth to ask what her mother had said, but closed it. She refused to play into his hands. After Mark got his hot hands on the book, it would give her time to grill her dear mother. Early on she decided her mother's memory lapses tended to benefit her and never anyone else. When her mother bet her an expensive skillet she couldn't make a hundred on every spelling test in the eighth grade, she somehow couldn't quite remember the details of the bet. Eventually, a cheap Teflon skillet showed up on her bed one day as a consolation prize.

"Why did you think it was okay to search the room?"

Mark's even voice didn't display any anger. Although most detectives would have, especially after repeatedly reminding her not to compromise crime scenes. He could have been asking if she had any decaf coffee for all the interest he displayed. Donna wrinkled her nose, surprised he hadn't acted the tiniest bit provoked.

"We were cleaning the room."

"You clean inside of suitcases?"

The way he said it made her actions sound felonious. Thanks to her mother, she was no better than a shoplifter. "No, but her suitcase could have been open." She suspected Mark could see through her as well as a picture window.

"Hmm." His hand stroked his chin as he spoke. "Your inn has to be the cleanest one around considering when I talked to you earlier you mentioned cleaning the room, even told me how neat J.E. was."

She wrestled with and overcame the temptation to slap her hand to her forehead while moaning *Duh*. "Ah, yes. So much is happening that it's easy to get confused." Her hand went up in an airy wave she'd seen more than one nurse use when asked about an undone task.

"Got it. It's your story, and you're sticking to it. Right?" He nodded slightly, but his lips remained in a firm line revealing nothing.

Why did the man have to go reasonable on her? "Okay." Her hands went up in mock surrender. "I didn't want Maria or Mom's help, but unfortunately, neither of them would leave in a prompt fashion, which explains why they all trooped into the room with me."

His index finger popped up. He gave her a long look. "Explain to me why you went into the room again?" His hand dropped back down to his side.

"Seriously?" Her hands fisted at her side, a sign she was long past feeling guilty. "You know good and well what I was doing. You're always complaining about a lack of manpower. I decided on using woman power. Even you have to admit, I've helped you on previous cases. Besides, having a woman look at something brings a different perspective. Men view the scene through masculine eyes. The same scene observed by a woman can yield different clues, especially if the possible victim is a woman."

Her chin went up the slightest bit, feeling as if she'd made her case. In fact, it would be smart to have a man and a woman on every case. Like that would happen in Legacy. The city didn't even employ an animal control officer. The exit of the manufacturing jobs had caused a downsize or elimination of many civic positions. Despite the upswing in the economy, the positions were never reinstated. The police handled the mad dog or pig in the garden calls.

"What can you tell me with your feminine acuity?"

It was difficult to tell if Mark was toying with her since he kept his face so expressionless. He must show the same face to perps. Her skin flushed, and her eyes narrowed as her mind raced through the filing cabinets of her memory, looking for a right example.

"Well, ah, I knew by the way J.E. marched into the place shouting orders that she was neither depressed nor suicidal."

Mark's eyes displayed a spark of interest. "Why is that?"

"The woman walked with determination. She knew what she wanted and didn't want. No time was wasted on trying to charm Daniel, Maria, or me. When she demanded sherry, she expected it to happen."

"Hmm." Mark scratched his temple. "Sounds like someone I know." He flashed a brief smile before continuing. "How do you know she wasn't acting?"

"Honestly, I never considered it. Why would she bother to act for me? I don't think so. It was the same act for everyone if she was, and it never varied. If someone were depressed, they wouldn't have the motivation or the energy to keep up a front like that. Besides, her journal referred to the new life she would have on a tropical island with her former flame."

"Aha, the journal would not be female intuition." He grinned, assured he'd caught her in a trap.

"Maybe. The earlier doubts encouraged deeper investigation. When she left this morning to meet a friend, she had on her vixen ensemble. I knew immediately the friend wasn't a woman."

"Okay, I'll assume that was what she was wearing when we found her. How would that be different than what she'd wear to meet a woman?"

Did she have to spell it out for him? "If she were meeting a woman, she'd want to impress. She'd don expensive designer labels. J.E. would definitely have a handbag that cost more than a half dozen gourmet dinners."

"Should I ask?"

"To impress the woman friend with her success. Since she wasn't married, she couldn't go on about her marriage or children, but she did have a notable career. The best way to show it would be by visible signs such as clothes, shoes, and jewelry. Was she wearing any expensive jewelry?"

Mark's brow furrowed as he worked his chin side to side, making a slight clicking noise as his jaw rotated in and out of the socket.

Finally, he shook his head. "I don't know. Then again, I don't have the feminine observation powers you have. I can pull the report up and look. All I really know is that her sister should be in town to identify the body. She'll probably want to pick up the suitcase, too."

The expensive luggage loaded with numerous black outfits and one red nightie didn't concern her. "What about the notebook?"

"It's evidence. We'll keep it until the case is solved."

Donna wagged her index finger. "What you're not saying is you plan on not mentioning it."

Mark cleared his throat and then coughed. "I didn't say anything. I advise you to do likewise until we figure things out. If it is a murder, as opposed to a suicide, then the first place you look besides a disgruntled lover is family."

Why not vengeful chefs or restaurant owners? Obviously, they had more of a grievance against J.E., but the family might disagree.

Chapter Twelve

DONNA'S MOTHER BREEZED into the kitchen in a cloud of spicy perfume. She flashed a bright smile and wiggled her French manicured fingertips in a wave. "Hello, y'all. Are you waiting for little ol' me?"

Donna cut her eyes toward Mark to see how he took the self-assured tornado that was her mother. Mark's lips pressed together in a solid line as if preventing himself from saying anything, but his eyes twinkled with hidden mirth. If he wasn't going to say anything, Donna would.

"Did you bring back the book?"

Her mother's hand dipped into a floral tote and pulled out a sheaf of papers and the stenography pad. "I did better. I brought the transcript, too. There's some interesting reading in those pages." Cecilia arched her eyebrows.

Mark stepped forward and accepted the book. He glanced at Cecilia's ungloved hands. "I guess it would be pointless to dust the pad for fingerprints."

The implication that evidence may have been compromised rolled off her mother's shoulders. "You must be Mark, my daughter's sometime suitor."

"Mother!" She gave her mother a slight push. "I never said that!"

"I know. I know. But people talk." Her mother folded her arms and gave Mark a significant look.

The detective was already turning the pages of the transcript and too deep into the information to remark.

Her mother gave a dismissive sniff. "It's no wonder you aren't getting anywhere with this one."

"Mother." Donna glanced at Mark, who was still perusing the papers. "I wish you wouldn't say things like that." She angled her head to the man in question. Donna might be able to exercise some control over nurses and residents with a stern look, but she'd never had any impact on her mother. It could be because the woman who gave birth to her always considered herself in charge.

"I brought you some more profiles. I went back and reviewed all the flirts I got and looked for younger men like you told me."

Donna shuffled back a few steps. Could this be happening? Mark's eyes shifted back and forth as he read. An occasional snort or chuckle sounded, making her wonder what was on the pages.

"That girl, the one who died, she really had a way with words. Even though everything was written in shorthand, an underlying snarkiness is still there. Then, when she talks about a future with George, there is almost a girlish naiveté to her writing. Everyone knows George is a horndog, even if he's calling himself Sylvester now. He's probably played fast and loose with so many women he doesn't want them tracking him down."

Donna blinked. Did her mother just say *horndog*? Who had taken over her mother's body? "I think he changed his name to Sylvester to make the restaurant sound better. If he called it George's Backroom, he couldn't charge forty dollars an entrée."

Before her mother could reply, Mark spoke. "I appreciate the transcript. I think it gives me more direction. Thanks." He held up his hand as a form of leave-taking while heading for the back door. The growl of a car engine allowed her to track him. Donna peeked out the front window to watch the sedan maneuver out of the parking lot without any haste. "Whatever he read in that notebook wasn't a slam dunk. Otherwise, he'd use his siren when he left."

Her mother joined her at the window. "Anyone could have knocked her off. There was more than one person she annoyed. I would almost suspect her employer."

Donna tilted her head to one side. "Why would you suspect her employer? Better yet, who is her employer?"

Her mother continued to stare out the window. Her neighbors with their standard-sized poodle came into view. Her mother tapped on the window glass with her nail. "Aren't those the nosey neighbors who pretend to walk their dog to spy on everyone else?"

The men in question stared in the direction of the inn and waved, leaving Donna no recourse but to smile and wave back. Donna hooked her hand around her mother's arm and pulled her back away from the window. "I didn't say that exactly." She might have thought it, but she couldn't believe she'd been indiscreet enough to say something like that in front of her mother.

Her mother's shoulders went up in a shrug. "Not sure who said it. Could have been Maria, Daniel, or even that nice young man you hired."

"Tennyson? You've been talking to Tennyson?" She held up her hand. "Don't answer. I want to know who J.E. was actually working for, and why they might get rid of her."

"The newspapers her reviews are run in are owned by a media conglomerate. The man who owns them is that obnoxious fellow with the foreign accent."

"Mom, I know who you mean. It isn't a foreign accent. He's from Boston."

Her mother moved around the kitchen, rearranging items on the counter. Donna considered asking her to stop, but realized an argument might result, causing her mother to forget the vital information she was relating.

"Why would her employer want to get rid of her?" She held her hands at her side, fighting the desire to push her utensil barrel back in place by the stove where she liked it.

"Ah, that. J.E. wasn't following instructions. Their instructions included what restaurant to praise and which one to savage. She had to be subtle. A sudden change in her review style might raise questions."

Donna moved the major spices she had on the shelf above her stove back in the order she preferred, hoping her mother hadn't noticed her actions. She kept them in the order of most used, while her mother arranged them according to size. "Sounds to me like some people were buying good reviews."

"It could be. In the end, J.E. was pushing back. She had no desire to savage her former lover's restaurant. That's why she offered them the tidbit about Norelle's moving to escape their previous bad reviews. She offered them up as a sacrificial lamb to save her sweetheart and set up her new life." Cecilia pulled out the knives from the knife block and regarded them as if she'd never seen them before.

Not the knives—she needed to distract her mother. "I made turtle cheesecake the other day. It's frozen, but a few minutes in the toaster oven would warm it up. Would you like some?"

Her mother picked up the chef knife and regarded her with a slight smile. "I know what you're doing, but I'll stop for cheesecake." Cecilia carried the knife to the island as she climbed up on a stool.

Donna picked up the chef knife as she made her way to the fridge. "Why would the newspaper chain want to get rid of its top money maker? The media conglomerate should want someone who brings in the money."

Her mother watched her progress with avid eyes. "Are you going to use syrup on the cheesecake?"

"I could." She didn't think her dessert needed an extra flourish, but if it made her mother happy, she'd add it, probably dark chocolate. "What is your theory as to why the paper killed her off?"

"The woman wasn't following directions. It would be easy to replace her with some aspiring critic, considering how no one really knows what she looks like. For all we know, this could be the second or the third incarnation of J.E."

The frozen confection, clutched against her chest, chilled Donna. Her mother's suggestion allowed her to ignore the cold somewhat. "You might have something there. I've heard about famous writers having ghost writers write for them because the publishing house wants to put out several books at once. It has something to do with the publisher actually owning the author pen name. Maybe this could be the case with the paper. Killing is over the top when they could cancel her contract." A fantasy involving her presenting the information that closed the case took shape in her mind. Even though J.E.'s death must have been premeditated, someone in the vicinity had done the deed.

She centered a piece of cheesecake on a pie pan, then added a second piece. Her mother wouldn't want to eat alone. When the toaster oven bell dinged, Donna moved the slightly cool cheesecake to two saucers she'd prepared with twin drizzles of syrup.

"Mom, you'll be my guinea pig today. I have both dark chocolate and hazelnut syrups on the saucer. You can tell me which one complements the cheesecake the best."

"Someone has to do it." Her mother grinned and moved to get

forks and napkins. "You really should invite me over more often. I could be a big help."

Donna knew *big help* was code for *takeover*. "You already have with decoding the notebook. You've pretty much nailed the case down with the information about her employer."

Her mother wrinkled her pert nose. "I don't know. So many people could have done the deed. We all know how George is, though he may not have been that way in the past. J.E. finds out that not only is her former flame the unfaithful sort, but he just stuck a pin into her personal dream bubble. It could have been like that old movie I saw the other night. The man planned to kill his wife for the insurance money and so he could marry his gal on the side. He loaded her drink with her prescription medicine. Too much would kill her and would look like an accidental overdose. The wife overheard the plans and switched drinks." Cecilia stretched her arm out and held her fingers together as if holding a wine glass. "It could have been one of those fancy toasts like they do at weddings. Once J.E. realized she drank the wrong glass, she probably headed to the hospital for help."

Neither she nor Mark had told Cecilia where J.E. had been found, but she was going the right direction if she were heading to the hospital. The hospital had bought land on the edge of the city limits to allow it to serve Legacy and nearby Colombo, which billed itself as the city that used Cristoforo Colombo's real name and correct spelling, as opposed to the anglicized version.

Donna tried to think of herself as J.E., an abrupt critic, who had a secret romantic side. It wasn't as big of a stretch as she thought it might be. She couldn't see the woman running from the scene. Calling 911 immediately would be the best course of action. If her intent was to murder her former flame, she'd at least make another attempt even if it killed her doing so. It would be a romantic tragedy, if killing your faithless lover counted as romantic. In the end, she couldn't logically make it work.

"No, I don't think so. J.E. struck me as more of a fail-safe person. She wouldn't do anything that could go so horribly wrong."

Her mother savored her first bite of cheesecake by closing her eyes. "This is wonderful." She used her fork to push a second piece through the syrup and lifted it to her mouth. A pleased smile tugged the corners of her mouth. "The chocolate works well, not overly sweet. I should try the hazelnut, too."

Her mother devoured her piece while Donna mentally listed who might want to kill her missing guest. Her mother reached for Donna's untouched cheesecake at the same time the uniformed officer entered the kitchen and spoke.

"Have any of you seen Detective Taber?"

Donna's hand covered her mouth. She hadn't even remembered the man's presence in her back bedroom. Whatever was in the notebook had caused Mark to leave in a hurry, but the canny individual that he was, he'd acted as if nothing was wrong. Sly, she had to admire that in the man. If she mentioned Mark left without bothering to talk to the officer, it would only make him sound ditzy.

Her mother looked up, interested, possibly ready to answer. Donna jumped in before Cecilia could. "He had to answer an emergency call. Detective Taber asked me to tell you he'd meet you at the station. Find any clues in the room?"

The officer laughed. "I was warned you'd try to wiggle information out of me."

Her mother joined in the laughter. "You're too smart for anyone to fool. Would you like some cheesecake before you leave?"

Her mother was good at giving away her food.

The officer glanced at her untouched plate, before making his excuses. "I had breakfast, and even had a second breakfast after I arrived here." He patted his stomach. "I might get fat if I stay any longer."

Her mother snorted in disbelief. "A nice-looking young man like yourself has nothing to worry about. You can go ahead and have a piece with no worries." She pulled Donna's saucer across the island to an empty stool beside her, moving the clean fork beside the plate.

The man sat without any more coercion. "I'll eat this, but then I really have to go."

Cecilia nodded in agreement. "Totally understand. Being an officer is hard work."

Donna returned to her seat convinced her mother would try to extract information from the unsuspecting man. He expected her to ask prying questions, not her cheerful, elderly mother. There really shouldn't be anything in the room she hadn't already uncovered, but the man could have information about J.E. that Mark neglected to tell her. With that in mind, she placed her elbows on the island and leaned forward so as not to miss a word.

"I imagine women just swarm around you, being a policeman and all. There's something about a man in uniform."

The officer's Adam's apple bobbed as he made a hard swallow. Her mother might as well use a trowel to pack on the heavy praise. When would she get to the part about asking about J.E.?

The man flushed since it was hard to agree with a compliment without appearing conceited. The fresh-faced policeman with the hat-band hair did not strike her as a player. His earnestness reminded her more of a grade-schooler, the ones who were eager to please, not the ones who rifled through the teacher's desk.

"I bet working all the time, solving serious crimes…"

Oh good, her mother was finally getting to the point.

"…leaves you no time for a social life."

His fork scraped against the plate as he cleaned up the last bit of crust crumbs. "You're right. Social life is a bit on the thin side."

Her mother made sympathetic sounds. Oh, she was good. Donna never had a clue the woman could play a man like a violin. Her dates probably didn't stand a chance.

"Aw, you poor thing." Cecilia held up her index finger. "These young girls don't have sense enough to appreciate a hard-working pillar of the community like yourself."

"So true." The officer nodded as he stared at his empty plate as if it had magically cleaned itself.

She curved her hand to cradle her face. The pregnant silence inserted itself as Cecilia pretended to think. Donna knew the woman planned minutes ago exactly what she would say. Her eyes blinked, and her face brightened as if an idea just occurred to her. Her mother straightened up and threw the man a wide smile. "I got it!"

"What?" Both she and the young cop spoke in unison.

Her mother held a finger up to her mouth and stalled, increasing the anticipation. Finally, Cecilia released a deep breath, then winked at her. *Good.* Here comes the big question after she'd lulled the man into a sense of complacency.

"An older woman would be understanding of the demands of your career."

The officer swallowed hard again and stood. "I need to go." He left so fast the back door slammed behind him.

Her mother clucked in disgust. "Not well played. I think he thought I wanted a date with him."

"Didn't you?" Donna reached across the island to gather the dirty dishes.

"Good heavens, no. I have no use for that puppy. I was trying to set you up."

Donna coughed, then attempted to clear the obstruction lodged firmly in her throat. It had to be composed of equal parts horror and disbelief. "Why?" She managed to force the word out.

"For your own good. You don't even have to go out with the man. It should be just enough to light a fire under your detective."

"He's not my detective."

"I know. That's the problem."

Chapter Thirteen

DONNA SQUIRMED ON the leather seats of the luxury sedan. The dreaded double date was uncomfortable when she was seventeen, but one with her own mother topped the list of things to avoid. The silver-haired man beside her reached for her hand resting on the seat, which she pulled out of reach. Her mother's rationale for the date included getting her into Norelle's to snoop. A fake date would work since she had no desire to impress Henry with her intelligence and sparkling wit.

Henry elbowed her slightly since he failed to get her attention by grabbing her hand. "I appreciate Cici fixing us up. She must have realized I was too much of a man for a woman near my own age to handle." He added a broad wink to emphasize his point.

The hard edge of the car door bit into her hip. She'd scooted over as far as she could go to be out of the reach of her amorous date without jumping out of the car. The familiar shape of the local Baptist church came into view, which meant in two more blocks she could put distance between her and the aging Lothario.

The things she did to help solve a crime. She only hoped Mark appreciated the lengths to which she went. Norelle's did have good food and she needed to get a gander at their Wall of Death. The photo they had up might not even be the same woman who stayed at her inn. The car bumped into the parking lot where valet attendants swept open the car doors. *Escape.*

Cecilia and her date led the way into the restaurant with their heads angled toward one another as they conversed. Harmon, her mother's date, put out a hand to cup her elbow and guide her into the restaurant. It must have served as some type of male competition because Henry grabbed for Donna's arm again. Her elbow met his ribs. She ignored his grunt, but slyly commented, "As a much younger woman, I can walk on my own."

"Bet you could wrestle a few alligators, too."

Her date's grimace told the tale that he might be falling out of love with the idea of a younger woman, especially a strong one who could arm wrestle him and win. "Never wrestled a gator, but I hog-tied a few steers."

Her mother ruined her conversation ploy by interrupting, "What are you talking about? I doubt you'd know the difference between a steer and a heifer."

Really, Mom, you had to go there. Her shoulders went back at the remark. "You get better marbling of the meat with a heifer."

"You gotta love a woman who knows her steaks." Henry grinned, probably pleased that he could serve as her knight.

Donna, already irritated with her mother for the impromptu date, gave the man a grateful smile for rushing to her defense. The slight upward tilt of her lips must have served as a green light since he stepped closer and snaked an arm around her waist. The appearance of the suited restaurant host quelled her desire to accidentally step on her date's toes. While she wasn't holding out for a second date, she didn't want to attract attention. A woman brawling with her date tended to be memorable.

"Welcome to Norelle's." The host bowed and clicked his heels together. "You're in for a Cajun-style treat tonight. Would you like to start at the bar or do you have a reservation?"

Harmon perked up at the mention of reservation, but before he could say anything, Cecilia spoke. "Ooh, we'd love to see the bar. We've heard so much about it." She clapped her hands together in anticipation. "I can't wait."

So much for playing down their curiosity. Her mother's date put up a hand as if asking permission to speak.

"I made a seven o'clock reservation. The name's Jensen."

Cecilia patted her date's arm as if indulging a child. "We're only stopping in for a peek and a drink. I doubt they'll run out of food."

She nodded at Donna, who picked up the verbal baton. "I'd like to see the bar, too, especially the crystal skulls I've heard so much about." Her hand went up to her neck and rubbed it. Asking to see the photos would be too over the top. She'd heard of people saying exactly what they were going to do just to distract people, but that must have been in larger cities. In Legacy, people would remember if she asked about the Wall of Death. She'd make some excuse to go to the restroom later and then drift past the photos.

The four of them entered a dark bar lit by flickering candles and colored lights spotlighting the top-shelf liquors. A light under the counter gave the bartender a supernatural glow, making him into a mythical being of the dark kingdom. A low rumble of a masculine voice mingled with a girlish titter filled the room. Donna peered into the dark to no avail. Silhouettes of heads and shoulders melted away into blackness. How in the world did anyone see the photos? Perhaps they found some excuse to pop into the restaurant during the day.

Her lips twisted to one side as she swiveled her head side to side to figure out where the wall might be. The description said it faced the bar. Darkness enveloped the tables. The votive candles threw up a sliver of light, letting them know which tables were vacant or occupied. Donna stared in the direction of where the wall should be when a cell phone illumination reflected off the glass. Ah yes, the wall was revealed by someone's dissatisfaction with their date, caused by checking their cell phone for other stimulation.

Her date, who still had his arm around her, took the opportunity to whisper in her ear. "There's the crystal skulls you wanted to see."

He didn't need to whisper, but the place had that kind of feel to it, rather like the waiting room for purgatory. Two crystal skulls sat at different ends of the bar on lighted display cubes that threw up purple and pink light into the grinning heads. What should have been playful colors struck her as being somewhat sinister.

The four of them shuffled to a table in the dark. Henry used the lack of light as an opportunity to pull her even closer. His cologne almost choked her. It was past time to make her getaway. "I need to go to the powder room."

Cecilia, aware of her plans, volunteered to go with her. Henry called after them. "What about your drinks?"

Her mother answered. "Shiraz wine."

Donna hadn't come for food or drink, but for information and refused to take the time to decide if she should go with wine or a cocktail. "You can order for me."

Glad to be away from her presumptuous date, she shuffled in the direction she saw the reflection. Her mother latched onto her arm, telling her, "No wonder you aren't dating. You could be a little more accommodating."

"No, I couldn't. I have no clue who this man is. I didn't agree to a date. I'm merely here to check out the wall. Who knows? I might become nauseated and have to leave unexpectedly." Even though she had made the plan up on the spot, it already appealed to her.

Another woman was using a flashlight app on her mobile to

examine the pictures. Her mother pulled out an LCD flashlight from her purse and flicked it on. The strong beam not only illuminated the photos, but also a nearby kissing couple.

"Stop with that light!" a man complained, while her mother fiddled with the flashlight.

"I have a low beam here somewhere." She stabbed at the light, somehow lessening the strength of the beam. "That's better."

"I'd say so. You could practically do surgery with the high setting. Shine it on the pictures." The light shined on the black-and-white pictures, showcasing each one for a few seconds. Dignitaries, celebrities, and heads of state graced the wall. Despite Cecilia's flashlight, shadows lurked around the photographs, making the images somewhat vague and indistinct. Finally, they got to the last photograph. A pleased woman with well-shaped eyebrows stared back at them.

"Is that the woman who checked into your inn?"

"I don't know. It's hard to say. I never saw her happy face. She always seemed to have a pinched look as if she smelled something bad or had indigestion. Besides, even with your flashlight, it is still hard to recognize the people in the photos. I accept that the photo in front of me was a famous guitarist because I know that he died. I'm placing names to the pictures based on recent deaths. It would really help if I could see the pics in the light."

A presence slid up behind Donna, causing her top teeth to worry her bottom lip. She attempted to tamp down her ill ease. *We're in a public place where nothing can happen.*

"Can I be of help, ladies?"

It may have been their host, but she couldn't tell in the dark. Whoever it was, it was super creepy to slide up behind them. Her mother responded first by giggling.

"Goodness, you scared me coming out of nowhere like a wraith or something."

The man gave a slight chuckle. "You aren't the first to mention it. Are you enjoying our selection of dead celebrities?"

Donna tapped the photo her mother still had illuminated. "Who is this?"

The height and voice indicated a male employee. A triangle of white could have been his shirt. The man coughed. "I don't know who that one is. I understood that the portraits were of famous people, but this person I don't know."

That would really burn J.E.'s butt, if she wasn't already dead. Did the man truly not know her? He could be the owner, who had been incinerated by a previous review. His mention of not knowing who she was could be the final stab at the woman who tried to bury him and his restaurant.

The flashlight flicked off. Her mother reached for her hand. "We better get back to our table. Our dates will wonder what happened to us."

"You're right." She agreed for the anonymous man's benefit, but still contemplated slipping out through the kitchen. "Are you really attached to your date?"

"Mercy me, no. I think we should still stay, though. I like to think I taught you better manners."

Donna sniffed. It didn't take a psychic to know she'd have to endure another hour or two of Henry. "Okay. Still, I think you owe me."

"I don't understand you. I've provided you with a night out on the town."

"Jasper is a better date. I could be browsing brunch menus. I've been thinking about offering a Sunday brunch. Just special occasions right now, like Mother's Day or Easter, but once I retire from the hospital, it could be a regular thing."

Her mother clucked her tongue in dismay until she bumped into a table. "Ouch."

Donna steered them in the direction of the bar, knowing their table was close by. Her mother placed her head close to hers. "I want you to be as happy as your father and I were. You're not getting any younger."

It was a somewhat sweet sentiment if she hadn't added on the age thing. "I'm glad you and Dad were so happy together, but not everyone gets married or has kids. Just accept the fact that cooking makes me content. Running the inn fulfills me. There's no reason for you to turn over your boyfriends to me. If you don't like them, there's no reason I would. Let's go see what Henry ordered for me. I think that will tell the tale."

They could hear the men talking before they could recognize them by candlelight.

"I'm not sure about your date, Harmon, but mine is playing hard to get. I do love a challenge."

Her mother elbowed her and laughed. Wasn't there some contract about mothers always being on their offspring's side? Amusement at her discomfort didn't count. The tiny votive flame highlighted their dates' noses, chins, and cheekbones, but left their eye sockets shadowed and ominous. The two could have been hosts for a horror movie festival.

Donna slid into her seat as her mother did likewise. "What did you order for me?"

The waiter appeared and placed a couple of short glasses in front of the men. A balloon goblet quarter filled with red wine went to her mother. The waiter held a tall glass garnished with a lime slice and a maraschino cherry. "Long Island Iced Tea?"

Henry pointed to Donna as if there was any question. *Yay Henry,* you never disappoint when it comes to being predictable. The "I told you so look" she shot her mother was totally wasted since she couldn't see her mother's expression in the dim light.

A waiter appeared by their table with a small penlight. "Let me guide you to your table."

Donna made a mental note to forget her drink, which served as a staple in every college town restaurant where getting drunk often served as a goal. The other three scooped up their drinks while Donna held her right hand down low letting everyone assume she had the drink. The tiny light swept the table, settling on her untouched glass.

"Looks like someone forgot their drink." The helpful server picked up the drink and held the sweating glass up. Donna reached for it. As her fingers closed around the chilled glass, she considered the possibility of tripping, spilling the drink, and getting the crisp Chardonnay she should have ordered to be with.

The waiter joked as he ushered them into the better-lit restaurant. "Hard to get the party started without your drink."

No reason to explain to the chirpy individual that no party would be starting. However, when it came to solving a murder, that would be a different story.

Chapter Fourteen

CECILIA SLIPPED OFF her shoes as soon as she entered the inn. Donna, who chose not to don feet-torturing heels, had no reason to abandon her footwear.

"Well, that didn't turn out the way I planned," Donna said. "I do appreciate your remark about my wayward teenage son who was sucking us both dry dealing with his legal issues."

"Yeah, that was a good one. I'm surprised Harmon didn't burn rubber getting out of there."

"We're lucky he stopped to let us out of the car as opposed to pushing us out while the car was still moving." The sound of girlish giggling emanated from the kitchen. "I suspect my troublesome *son* may be up to something."

They pushed the door open the tiniest sliver, revealing Winnie and Tennyson huddled around the blender along with a tub of vanilla ice cream, milk, and a bottle of root beer schnapps. Instead of using the shot glass, Tennyson poured the liquor directly into the blender.

Winnie bit her lip. "Do you think your employer will mind?"

The man gave a hoarse chuckle. "Of course not. We're like this." Tennyson held up two crossed fingers, which caused Donna to growl low in her throat. Her mother gave her a slight shove and hissed in her ear.

"The boy is trying to impress the girl by making her an alcoholic milkshake. It's rather sweet, in a certain way."

Was this her mother? "There is also the issue of underage drinking. Winnie may be twenty-one, but Tennyson isn't. Sweet doesn't involve wasting my root beer schnapps. I had to go into the next county to buy it since none of the stores stock it here."

"You need the schnapps why?

An alcoholic root beer float had become her guilty pleasure. "Maybe I don't need it, but some days it sure does hit the spot."

When she turned back to spy on Winnie and Tennyson, they were both gone, along with their milkshakes. Donna and Cecilia entered the kitchen. Her mother, ever the one to point out the positive, remarked, "At least they put the ice cream and milk away."

The blender was in the sink. A few quick steps carried her to the holiday cabinet where she hid the schnapps while she kept most of the other liquor in a locked cabinet. The wine stayed in the basement, which was also locked. She grabbed the longneck bottle and put it on the counter with intentions of moving it to the locked cabinet.

"Oh goodie. We get adult beverages." Her mother clapped her hands together as if she'd been offered a Popsicle.

Oh well, it might do them both good. She twisted the water on and rinsed out the blender. "I would have suspected you would be full after wolfing down all that crawfish etouffee.

"Please." Her mother climbed up on a stool and wrinkled her nose. "I barely ate half of that when I made up the story about your alleged son. Harmon and Henry headed for the restroom and came back with some urgent meeting they had to attend. Somehow, they forgot that they had both mentioned being retired on their profiles."

"True. I suspected they might do as much. That's why I shoveled down the shrimp and grits. It was excellent." She made a smacking sound with her lips. "Even if I did eat it in record time."

The ice cream scooper slid effortlessly through the frozen cream. After piling several scoops into the blender, she added the liquor in a long pour.

"No shot glass? No milk?"

"Nope. Found out today my mother's affinity for lying. I'm trying to deal with the shock."

Cecilia made a face since little could be heard over the blender's grinding motor. Once Donna clicked it off, she grabbed her chance. "Come on, what did I do that was so wrong? You wanted to get inside Norelle's. I provided a way. People lie all the time to get along."

In theory that might be true, but Donna didn't think of her mother that way. "I never knew you to lie before this." She poured a thick stream of alcoholic root beer float into each glass and pushed one toward her mother.

"Ha, shows how much attention you paid in the past." Cecilia took a sip and wiggled her eyebrows. "Santa Claus, Easter Bunny, Tooth Fairy, your surprise birthday party, and that time you didn't want to go to school because that one girl ridiculed you."

"You called and told the principal I had chicken pox." Of course, that revelation ended up with Donna in a doctor's office and her mother getting an all clear doctor's note for her return to school. "Yeah, I guess you've been a liar from way back when. I'd think you'd be better at it by now."

Her mother snorted as she chugged down a quarter of her drink. The glass thumped on the counter, and her mother cleared her throat. "You almost choked me. I'm just fine at lying. Besides, they're only white lies that don't hurt anyone. They are the grease that allows people to live together in relative harmony."

It was a valid point, especially considering all the fake regulations Maria made up in an effort to keep guests in check. "Yeah, I expect people to do the right thing, but discovered most don't know what the right thing is. Maria made up a slew of rules that imply a failure to follow them will result in some internal investigation by some legal body, possibly the FBI or the Health Department."

"Gotta love Maria. I knew there was something I liked about her the first time I met her."

The back door slammed, the slap of rubber-soled shoes followed, heralding the arrival of Tennyson carrying two empty glasses. He stopped and blinked, before slowly moving into the room.

Cecilia gave him an indulgent smile. "Did your little girlfriend go home?"

Whatever initial fright he'd had finding his employer and mother at the scene of the kitchen defilement vanished at the mention of Winnie. "She did. Wilhelmina worries about her grandfather."

The use of the full name signaled infatuation. It didn't necessarily mean Winnie invited use of her full name, but rather he chose to demonstrate their connection. Donna decided not to mention the schnapps and ice cream misappropriation. Normally, she'd have made them milkshakes sans the alcohol.

"Oh, look." She held up the empty bottle of schnapps and peered into it. "Where did it all go?"

The boy cringed, well aware it was confession time. "I may have used some of it." Tennyson's eyes dropped to his feet.

"Really? Just a teeny tiny bit?"

His thumb and forefinger stretched out about three inches. "Maybe more than a tiny bit."

"Hmm," Donna pretended to consider. "I guess you wouldn't mind buying me a new bottle then. It runs between $12 and $15."

"That much?"

"I didn't add on the expense of driving to the next county to obtain it."

The heel of his hand hit his head as he groaned dramatically. Cecilia slid off her stool and placed an arm around him.

"Don't worry. It would still be a cheap date. You have to make sacrifices in the name of love."

"I suppose." His head came up, and he plastered on a brave smile. "Winnie is worth it."

"Glad you feel that way." Donna motioned to the blender. "Surely you'll clean up after yourself in the name of true love."

Tennyson glanced at their glasses and looked as if he'd say something but picked up the blender instead. Discretion was how people stayed employed.

Her mother held out her wrist and twisted it slightly to peer at her delicate gold filigree watch. "It's getting late. Tonight may not have worked out the way we liked, but it was still something. You got any guests staying over?"

"Only a few. Sunday usually serves as departure day. Just as well since I have to work Tuesday. I'll get everyone out and the rooms cleaned before the next wave of visitors." Her shoulders drooped. "Geesh, I never seem to have a day off anymore. What about having some fun?"

"Depends on what you consider fun." Mark's mellow baritone came from the direction of the swing door. He stepped into the kitchen and nodded at Cecilia and Tennyson. "Heard you were out on a hot date."

Her mother shrugged while Tennyson refused to meet her eyes. It wasn't hard to figure out the information leak. She moved close to the counter and rested her right hand on the surface. Her nails drummed on the hard surface while she dropped her chin, trying to catch Tennyson's gaze. "I wonder where you heard such a thing?"

Her mother, who had been on the verge of leaving, boosted herself back up on a stool. "I think I'll stay a little longer. Things just got interesting."

The large bird, who appeared to have sung his heart out, made a sliding step toward the back hallway that would have made many a line dancer proud. He managed to do it while gazing off in another direction, too, probably to convince everyone he wasn't retreating. Donna knew better.

"Finish cleaning up before disappearing."

His head came up and threw a desperate glance in Mark's direction. She wanted to tell him there was no help there, but the man's face folded into a sympathetic expression. Her eyes rolled up in disgust. The man had a soft heart for everyone. "Let the boy live another day."

Her fingers stopped drumming. *Let him live another day*? He made her sound like a devourer of children. Outside of a little housework and maybe a sit-down talk about minding his own business, nothing traumatic would happen. "Did you swing by the inn for your information gathering moment?"

"I came by to thank your mother."

Cecilia acknowledged his appreciation. "You're most welcome. It wasn't all that much. I'm sure anyone else would have done it if they'd been conversant with Gregg shorthand. Fortunately, I keep my skills sharp by writing my own journal in shorthand."

It might do Donna some good to take a course in shorthand, in case she ever needed to read her mother's journal. It might be more scintillating than her own coded diary. "So, that's it? You came by to render your thank you and Tennyson tells you I'm out."

"Not exactly. He was worried about the two of you. Told me the two of you had cooked something up since there was much whispering and phone calls. The two of you got fixed up and some strange old geezers showed up to take you out."

Her mother snorted her feelings. "Old geezers, he got that part right. As for strange, they were the same old boring males who think changing the channel from bottom to top instead of top to bottom is a wild adventure."

Mark's eyes flickered from her to her mother and back again. "Your mother reminds me of someone." He waggled his eyebrows, leaving no doubt about who he meant. "Should I ask what you were up to on your date tonight?"

"It's my personal life. I don't see why you'd need to go sticking your nose in it."

"Fair enough." Mark leaned against the counter and folded his arms. "I mistakenly thought you might be investigating, and we could share info. Oh well." He yawned wide and stretched his arms over his head. "Better head home and hit the hay. Tomorrow is another day."

Donna inhaled deeply as she analyzed the detective's actions. She'd bet good money he wasn't the least bit tired, but was teasing her. It would be a shame if they didn't cooperate. The worst part was Mark didn't even assume she was on a real date. Her eyes narrowed as she surveyed the lounging man. No tight shoulders or forced smile, which would normally portray some anxiety. The man thought he had her in the palm of his hand.

Better yet, he might not be all that interested in her but had a definite preference for the free food she provided. Her brows knitted together. They never had been on one date, not one where she didn't make a meal. That made her little better than middle school girls who wrote the name of their crush all over their shoes, folders, and even hands without the slightest indication their affection was reciprocated.

It would serve him right to think someone might be interested in her. The last time he showed a twinge of jealousy was when Arnie showed up for the class reunion. Too bad the twinge was probably measured in nanoseconds. Donna had almost convinced herself to say nothing, but her telepathy apparently was on the fritz. Her mother spilled it all.

"Originally, we just wanted to get into the bar area to see the Wall of Death."

Mark pushed off from the table and took a stool at the island. He had the temerity to smirk at her before turning back to her mother with an attentive expression. "Did you see it?"

"Bits and pieces. I brought a flashlight. Good thing, too, since it was as dark as a cave in there. The only thing that was illuminated was the liquor bottles and the crystal skulls. Our intention was to check out J.E.'s photo or alleged photo and compare it to the actual guest."

"Well?" Mark glanced at Donna and left the question hanging since Cecilia had never seen the critic in the flesh.

"It was very dark. The flashlight created a glare, and there was the creepy guy who kept making strange remarks." Mark's eyebrows went up the same time a thought occurred to her. "Mom, did you get a good look at the man?"

Cecilia tilted her chin and stared down her nose, an expression that easily translated due to long associations as 'Are you kidding me?' but more often 'Are you crazy?'.

"No. Could barely see my own hand. Besides, the man kept out of the flashlight beam."

"That may have been intentional." Mark's finger went up beside his nose, an idiosyncrasy that meant he was working on a summation of the problem or clues.

Donna had already come to her own conclusion. "I thought at first the man was an employee, but he didn't really act like one, making sly remarks indicating J.E. was of no importance. Maybe he was the killer." The possibility had the hairs standing up on her arms faster than a polar vortex sweeping down the Carolina coast.

Chapter Fifteen

CECILIA GASPED AND hunched her shoulders forward as if trying to make herself a smaller target. She threw a fearful glance over her shoulder. The only frightening thing behind her was the open door of one of the maple cabinets. Donna knew it could put her eye out since she'd been told multiple times exactly that when she'd made the mistake of leaving a cabinet door ajar as a kid.

Mark held up his hand as if directing traffic with the palm facing out. "Wait. Before you go all movie of the week on me, I want to tell you what her sister Mary Ellen told me."

"Mary Ellen. Jane Ellen. Those two didn't have the most creative parents."

Her mother shook a warning finger. "We should at least listen to the good detective."

Donna fought the urge to point out the word *good* didn't necessarily go in front of *detective*, but she settled for a head bob instead.

"Mary Ellen identified her sister and admitted she'd been afraid something like this would happen for a while. J.E. had received death threats on a regular basis because of her scathing reviews. Mary Ellen expected her sister to be murdered."

Donna flapped her hand in the air. "Come on, people say they could kill someone for something they did about every five seconds. I'm sure Jane Ellen didn't take any of them seriously. It was part of the job, rather like being a referee."

"That's not what her sister said. Mary said her sister was depressed, even suicidal."

Donna shook her head violently. Hadn't they already discussed this and dismissed it? "You told me her body was found several yards from the car, that it appeared she was running away."

Mark's voice had a bit of a bite in it as he crossed his arms. "I'm well aware of what I said. Still, poison can make a person act irrationally. Perhaps she thought it would be a quiet death and the pain caused her to change her mind."

Before Donna could blow holes in his flimsy theory, Cecilia bounced up and down, reminiscent of a game show contestant. "Did you even read the transcript I typed? Even with a lack of articles and antecedents, the journal still glowed with hopeful anticipation. The woman was finally going to have the life she wanted."

Her experience with the veteran detective suggested the man could not be easily swayed once he drafted a deduction. "What changed your mind?" she asked.

Mark managed a sheepish smile. "Hate to admit it, but local gossip. One of the patrol officer's cousins is a hairdresser and hears all the gossip. Apparently, Sylvester popped the question and not to J.E. This could result in her thinking that magnificent life she'd planned for herself in the Bahamas had died a sudden death. Consider she no longer has a career, since she can't taste the food. The paper chain is pushing her to post fraudulent reviews. The only love of her life proposed to another woman."

"Yeah," Donna agreed, but hated doing so. Something about the scenario didn't feel right. "Most people agree that Sylvester, or George, or whatever he wants to call himself can be self-serving. The timing of this proposal sounds suspect."

"You're right." Her mother straightened and took on the slightly regal air she normally donned when she was certain of something. "As you know, those two have lived together a few years short of forever. I always figured Linona was the one holding back. She didn't want the possibility of splitting half her holdings. Then there was the issue with the man catting around. Why would he suddenly propose?"

Before Mark or Donna could offer probable reasons, her mother continued. "I think he was holding out for a good review from J.E. and was willing to play the boyfriend angle as long as he could to get it. Once the critic turned up dead, he's anxious to get married. Sounds to me like he's buying himself an alibi."

Personally, Donna never saw the appeal of Sylvester or his entrees. They were all show, with a snow pea curved around three quarter-size medallions of meat and a curl of ginger on the rim of the plate. No wonder people trotted over to The Croaking Frog for a real meal. "Not sure what Sylvester has to offer. His dishes are 90 percent pretension. He leads those who want to be led with tales about winning various awards. At least Janice's restaurant has been on television."

Her mother and Mark both laughed.

"What?" She lifted up her open hands with the palms facing one another and shook them. "Is it unreasonable for a person to want a decent sized portion entrée and for it to be tasty?"

Her mother winked at her. "It's not the food we're talking about, but the man. Plenty of women lap up the chef's arrogance. He has them believing he's very important in the culinary world."

Donna's hands dropped to her side, she sighed, and finally shot her hands into her hair, lifting it from her neck before letting it fall again.

Janice's distinctive text chime sounded, causing Donna to pull out her phone to scan it. "It's Janice. She wants to know if J.E. is really dead or if this is all a publicity scam?"

Mark grimaced. "It won't hurt her to wait for information like everyone else. What were you saying about Sylvester?"

"There have to be some awfully stupid women in this town. Oh, I know there are. It takes incidents like this to remind me." She held up one index finger as she gathered her thoughts. "Now the prevailing theory is she killed herself?"

"It has some merit," Mark concluded and stared off in the direction of the empty coffee pot. It didn't take psychic skills to get the message. However, since he hadn't shown a sliver of concern about her being out with another man, he could do without coffee. Besides, it would keep him up all night.

Her mother came from the kinder, gentler school of thought since she slid off her stool and strolled to the coffeemaker. "Where do you keep the grounds? It's obvious Mark is dying for a cup of Joe."

Typical. Her mother felt the need to look after any male in her vicinity. She opened several cabinets and closed the standing door in her hunt. Mark shot Donna a knowing look. Perhaps he gauged that her mother would fold before she did. If so, he read Cecilia well.

"It's in the freezer, which should be unlocked." Her mother busied herself with making coffee while Donna pointed out the obvious elephant in the room that everyone had overlooked. "Who's her beneficiary?"

Mark waggled his eyebrows. "Do you think whoever inherits knocked her off?"

"It has happened before."

"It could have if the beneficiary were forty-two as opposed to being two. Her niece, Sue Ellen, is the sole beneficiary."

While Sue Ellen might be out of the running, her mother was still a suspect. Of course, it would mean the woman had to be in town the entire time. "What about the mother?"

Mark moved his chin side to side, popping his jaw. "I'm not going to totally rule her out. I have people checking on her. While she's unremarkable, what is interesting is how little J.E. is paid for being a critic extraordinaire. There isn't a great deal to leave Sue Ellen."

"Okay." She'd heard that the high-profile jobs such as airline attendants and television reporters made less than teachers. Everyone knew teachers made barely enough to get by. "What about the company she works for taking out an insurance policy on her? She's their intellectual property. Losing her, for whatever reason, would hurt their bottom line."

Mark glanced her way, then stared at the convection oven, obviously mulling over the possibility. Cecilia delivered a cup of black coffee that Mark accepted with a grin.

"Haven't you watched any of those news magazine programs? Just the other day, one was on about this woman and her three children who lost their home after her husband died in a freak accident while the company he worked for had him insured for a million dollars." Her mother raised her voice. "One million dollars!"

"I think he heard you the first time." Although, it was hard to tell since Mark hadn't blinked or anything. Donna decided to play the devil's advocate in case the detective was coherent. "How did they get the man to sign the paperwork?"

Her mother, understanding her part, spoke a little louder. "They had him sign papers when he started work. They told him the insurance was standard. It really is when the company is hiring high-wage earners with all sorts of know-how. If they vanished overnight, the company would be in a world of hurt. The best way to fix that is hiring someone else equally talented and expensive. That's where the insurance policy comes in."

"They were already paying a high salary. Why the insurance policy?"

Her mother's lips tipped up in an appreciative smile, meaning she'd asked the right question.

"That's what the television reporter asked. The company rep talked about losing money while they did a job search, and how it wasn't easy to find someone with the exact qualifications. The reporter had done his homework and found out the man was replaced from within the company. No job search happened. They also had insurance policies on everyone in the company, including the janitor. The reporter concluded that with a large company, it was a safe bet that someone would die per year, sometimes more than one person. The company cashes in without any of the funeral expenses a family would have."

"That's just *criminal.*" Donna emphasized the last word, wondering what had Mark's attention. He hadn't even touched the coffee he wanted.

He gave them both a long-suffering look. "Stop with the dog and pony show. You've given me something else to think about. I should have known better. Murder is never easy. It's certainly not simple. It also makes me wonder why Mary Ellen was so quick to accuse her sister of suicide."

Daniel would never do that to her, but maybe her brother knew her much better than Mary Ellen did her sister. "Could be that the two of them didn't talk all that much. The woman might be shocked to know about J.E.'s potential plans. There could have been a reason she didn't tell her sister. Maybe too much besides sibling rivalry."

Her mother hummed her agreement while Mark shook his head. He held up his coffee cup. "Any chance I could get this in a to-go cup?"

What did he think this was? The fast food drive-thru? "I have a thermos you can use, but I expect it back. I bought it because it's guaranteed to keep liquids hot for five hours."

"Good. I have a feeling I'll be up for more than five hours. That's the problem with talking to the two of you, you stir up more possibilities. No matter how zany some of your theories are, they could be possible. My thirty plus years of police work has taught me never underestimate the sheer absurdity of the criminal mind. This could be something not directed at J.E., which means the killer could kill again."

Cecilia shot him a look that would have caused Donna to scamper for a hiding place when she was younger. "It could be a woman."

Donna rolled her eyes. Only her mother would fight for women to be considered equally deadly as the male gender.

"I don't. It's a figure of speech."

Even though Donna had previously been irritated with the man, she now took pity on him. She'd witnessed on more than one occasion her mother talking circles around her father, who gave up fast, probably confused about what they were originally discussing. Might as well get the man the thermos cup while he still had his sanity. A quick root through the drawers unearthed the cup she needed.

Mark accepted the cup, filled it, and capped it before holding it up as a departing signal. "See you lovely ladies tomorrow."

The bell jangled as he left. Donna glanced at the clock. "I'd better lock the door."

Her mother picked up her purse and retrieved her keys. "I better get moving, too. Smart idea with the thermos cup. It will make him return to bring it back."

"Yeah." No need to explain she never had any issues with Mark coming back. He reminded her of a stray dog always sniffing around for food. Donna rounded the island and hugged her mother. "Thanks for scaring up the escort to get us into Norelle's. Personally, I think we could have brought in Jasper and Loralee as our dates since it was so dark. Speaking of Loralee." She shaped her voice until it was a wheedle. "It would be grand if you could keep her. I can't handle two dogs, the inn, and work first shift. I can't ask anyone else since they all have jobs. Tennyson has to go to school."

Her mother gave her a suspicious stare. The woman could always see through her lies.

"I'll keep her this time since you have so much going on, but…" she paused on the word making certain Donna understood, "…this will not be a regular thing."

"Of course not." Donna turned, making sure her mother couldn't see her crossed fingers. "I know a dog is the last thing you need in your active social life.

Her mother snapped her fingers, waking the basset hound. Loralee staggered to her feet and followed. "That's right. I don't have time to fuss over a dog, especially one that someone has already put aside."

The two of them walked out the back door, triggering the security light that irritated her neighbors. The motion-sensitive light created a small circle of light in the parking lot. If a person parked strategically, as her mother had, there was no reason to ever enter a dark car. The woman bent and fondled the dog's ears. Even though the two of them were silhouettes, she could tell Loralee held her head up in an adoring pose, one she never shared with Donna. When the elderly dog jumped up on her bed last night, she hadn't the heart or the energy to push her off. If her mother didn't take the dog, she didn't know what she would do with the canine. An idea so perfect in its irony bloomed fully formed. Her hand covered her mouth in case she made the mistake of laughing aloud.

Chapter Sixteen

THE HIGH-PITCHED VOICE in the dining room caused Donna's lips to tip up as she cracked an egg on the rim of the metal mixing bowl. Most of her guests had left by Sunday afternoon, but a few had elected to stay, including Josephina Lee and her granddaughter, Scarlett. No matter how stiff the woman acted, it was obvious she adored her granddaughter. It only made sense she'd do whatever she could to please her.

Donna's eyes cut to the clock, checking the time. Maria wasn't coming since there were only four actual guests. If she couldn't whip up food for four guests, Tennyson, and herself, she had no right running a B and B.

The recent death of J.E haunted her thoughts. It was odd that the sister never came to the inn. True, the police carried out all of J.E.'s possessions and might hold them for evidence, but if something ever happened to her mother or brother while vacationing, she'd fly to wherever they had been in a heartbeat. She'd also grill anyone who came into contact with them. Not even coming by to walk the path her sister last took struck Donna as cold.

The timer burbled, reminding her the pastries and croissants she'd put in the oven were warm. Normally, pastries didn't go with a country breakfast on the menu, but she'd made a mistake of excluding them and had *two* guests mention the fact in their reviews. Apparently, everything was wine and roses, except for the lack of a cheese Danish.

The back door slammed accompanied by a long, mournful bay. It sounded like her mother had arrived with Loralee. Now all she had to do was needle Tennyson into action. Where was he? The juices and water along with the bread baskets and butter needed to go out.

"Hmm, something smells good." Cecilia strode into the room with her floral scarf trailing behind her like a banner. "If I'd known you could cook, I wouldn't have wasted my time fixing you breakfast all those years."

Loralee rushed past them, hit the swinging door at a lope and passed through it. Donna's eyes followed the dog and remained on the still moving door as she answered her mother. "From what I remember, we always had cereal." Any cooking talent she possessed did not come from the maternal side of the family.

"I know. You could have poured it yourself." Her mother wrinkled her nose at what she perceived to be a witty remark.

"Could you tap on Tennyson's door? He's supposed to be helping me."

Her mother cleared her throat. "You may have noticed I'm on time, dressed, and ready to help. Just think, I could have been your assistant instead of…"

A moan arrived before Tennyson did. He followed a few seconds later with his eyes glued to the phone in his hand. "Why did she throw me away like I didn't matter?" He jerked his head up to stare at Donna.

His reddened eyes and nose told the story. Her mother, who never heard of boundaries, leaned over and stared at the phone. "I see that nice girl went back home—oh, maybe she wasn't so *nice*—to her *boyfriend.*"

Tennyson groaned at Cecilia's summation. His wrinkled clothes appeared as if he had slept in them, and his shaggy hair looked worse than usual.

"Mother, you get to help serve today."

Her mother brightened and snapped a salute. "Aye, aye."

"We're not on a ship. You have a special assignment since Tennyson is going through a personal crisis."

"Pouring coffee? Slicing coffee cake?"

Donna shook her head, wondering if sending her mother out on assignment was her best bet. "All right." She held up her index finger. "There's a little girl out there named Scarlett who has never, ever had a pet."

"That's tragic!"

"I agree." She arranged the filled bread baskets on a tray and presented them to her mother. "Give each table a basket. When you get to Scarlett's table casually mention that the dog she met the other day is going to be put down. By the way, Loralee headed into the foyer. It's best you locate her before the emotional hard sell."

Cecilia's eyebrows arched at the pronouncement. "Telling a girl a dog will die if she doesn't adopt it isn't breakfast conversation."

"Would you like to keep the dog?"

Her mother inhaled and rocked back on her heels before answering. "She's a bed hog and someday I might…"

Donna held up her hand. "Too much information. Take out the bread, then come back for the juices. I'll see what I can do about Tennyson."

Just the mention of his name caused the boy to wipe his eyes. "Why did she leave me?"

"She didn't live here. It was only a visit." Donna hadn't noticed any great bond between the two of them, but she knew enough not to mention it.

"I know." He sniffed as Cecilia barreled into the kitchen, grabbed the juice tray, and added her two cents.

"It wasn't like it was a great love affair. You were obsessed with her. That's all. Don't go all stalker on us."

Tennyson blinked. No doubt the boy was in shock. Similar remarks were part of her heritage. When Donna's fiancé dumped her, a teenaged Daniel threatened to hunt him down and work him over. Her mother had remarked he could have done them the courtesy of showing his true colors before the wedding deposits were put down.

Her mother's remark had her thinking all the way through the bacon, hashbrowns, and western omelets. Practical people accept people who often don't love them back. Obsessive ones don't. What if whoever poisoned J.E. had no connection to her, but resented her connection to Sylvester? Tennyson whined through her entire meal preparation about never falling in love again.

She rolled her eyes. Why couldn't Daniel be here to dispense some male wisdom? Her mother might come back and slam the boy with another comment that might have him chugging a bottle of pills. Obviously, her mother could work on her sensitivity when she wasn't playing the part of a southern belle.

"Ah," she started, then stopped, never having had this conversation with a hurting male. "You have a great deal going for you. Winnie didn't spend enough time getting to know you to discover it."

"Really?" He lifted his head and managed a breathy gulp. "Name one."

Drat. She should have seen that one coming. "You were the mysterious rebel that Winnie decided to get involved with even though she knew she had a solid, boring boyfriend back home."

Tennyson pushed his meager chest out and shoulders back. "What makes me mysterious?"

There was no way she could win at this. Cecilia ducked in, grabbed the plates, and grumbled. "No luck finding the dog," then vanished again.

A prick of unease needled her. Too bad, it didn't come with specific instructions such as *this is for a missing dog*, or *this shot of apprehension is for the murderer*. Although her discomfort came from not knowing what to say, for once, she could use one of her mother's hold-everything remarks. "You're a philosophy major. I bet she doesn't know anyone else who is. All her friends are probably into business, nursing, or one of those practical fields that guarantee a job. You, on the other hand, live on the wild side of possibly, living in a cave or a dilapidated shack by the railroad yards."

She should have stopped when she was ahead. Tennyson's new-found pride sagged and buckled like his posture. He bent at the waist, cradling his head in his hands.

"No wonder she left. I'm going to be a homeless person."

Her mother ran into the kitchen, bug-eyed and her breath labored. "That woman out there is crazy. I'm not sure how you do it. I quit!" Her mother suited her actions to her words by picking up her purse and walking out the back way.

She was gone before Donna could point out that she hadn't hired her, which meant she couldn't, in theory, quit. A heavy hand hammering on the swinging door caused it to tremble and swing inward, exposing a red-faced Josephina and her tearful granddaughter.

What was this? Friday the 13th?

"Who was that woman who made my darling Scarlett cry?" The woman trembled with outrage.

Donna saw all sorts of legal action brought against her and the inn. A convenient lie that would cover whatever bizarre thing her mother said or did escaped her for the moment. "That was my mother. She wants to help. Sometimes, she's a bit too plain spoken."

Josephina huffed her opinion about the plain-spoken part.

"She really does mean well." Goodness, she'd gone about as far as she could. "She hasn't been the same since my father died."

Josephina wilted some, and her voice gentled, becoming less like an avenging angel's. "She's a widow. Poor thing."

"She was worried about Loralee, too. The dog is a bone of contention between a divorcing couple. No one wants her, so she'll probably be put down."

"What a shame. The children always suffer in a divorce."

Scarlett looked up at her grandmother. "Like me. Is Loralee suffering like me?"

"Hush, sweetheart, we don't need to air our dirty laundry." Josephina gave her granddaughter a small pat.

"Why would we air dirty laundry?"

Tennyson used the confrontation to vanish, leaving Donna with no one to clear the breakfast dishes. She was tempted to call him back but didn't. Let the poor puppy lick his wounds. She wished she'd taken the time to wallow in her misery when she found herself alone at the altar years ago. If she hadn't hardened her heart and been all work afterward, she might not be running this place alone. Truthfully, she probably wouldn't be running the place at all. It would be a hard sell to convince a husband of the benefits of running a B and B. It was up there with being a philosophy major.

The metallic rattle of the dog leashes resulted in Loralee trotting into the kitchen leaving an acrid cloud of eau de dog flatulence trailing her as she searched for the origin of the *walk* sound.

Josephina wrinkled her nose as the basset padded by.

The woman waved a hand in front of her nose. "I assume this is the dog your mother was talking about."

Donna shook her head, not even daring to breathe. Mark had warned her the dog's farts were toxic, but she had no clue.

Josephina headed for the foyer holding her nose. "Good luck finding a home for that gas factory."

The muffled sound of Josepehina's voice almost made her laugh, but the reality of the situation stamped out any humor. Loralee and Jasper's nails scratched on the linoleum as they did a canine happy dance once they had found Tennyson and the leashes. A walk would do the three of them some good. Tennyson's tall form passed the kitchen windows. He put up a hand as if aware of her observation. Hers went up in response. He'd left without a jacket, which wasn't a good thing considering his state of mind. Depressed people often caught colds and chills faster than happy individuals.

BY ONE IN the afternoon, everyone had checked out including Scarlett and her grandmother, without bothering to ask about Loralee. Count it a miracle if a review didn't show up with a mention of a crazy lady who made little girls cry. Tennyson could have handled the situation with more flare. She should have told him he was good with children and dogs, but college co-eds usually weren't looking for the dog whisperer.

Whenever a block of free time presented itself, she cooked ahead. Cheesecakes, quiches, even the appetizers froze well. Two rooms upstairs needed to be cleaned, but she wouldn't have guests for three more days. The place was lonely and empty. It might be one of the last good days before cold weather arrived, even though the leaves fluttering on the trees showed no signs of falling. How long could Tennyson walk the dogs? After dithering over whether she should wait for a couple more minutes longer, she locked the front door. It would be an excellent time to go visit A Little Bit of Paris Café and possibly shake some pertinent information out of the help.

The sun shone, making the idea of a cup of coffee on the outdoor patio appealing. For once, she wouldn't analyze the coffee or study the menu for possible items she could add to her rotation. It would be her turn to act like a tourist and make pithy comments, if only in her head, as people passed by.

The light traffic allowed her to make the trip faster than previously. No irate detective to stop her and no impulsive kisses to shut him up either. The mystery of the dead critic haunted her, too. Suicide didn't make sense. n angry chef could be the culprit. That would mean four suspects, including her friend, Janice. Although Janice had no reason to be angry since The Croaking Frog had never been reviewed. Janice's place could take a drop in customers due to a bad review.

If Fate was trying to be mysterious, she must have been juggling and dropped a ball. Donna blinked. She couldn't believe it! Right in front of the Little Bit of Paris's daily special sign, Sylvester and Linona sat at one of the black wrought iron tables, holding hands. The bright sun picked out the wrinkles in Linona's face. Still, hers was a happy face. Somehow, the thought of being engaged to a womanizer didn't repel her. If Sylvester was equally delighted, he forgot to inform his eyes. The crow's feet around them tightened, matching the furrows on his forehead.

It was no trick figuring out who was happier about the engagement. Linona waved her left hand around as if trying to rid herself of a swarm of flies or to show off her ring. The server, the same girl who was there the other day, didn't act impressed. The downward eyebrows and tight mouth suggested other emotions and none pleasant, but then it could have been a long day for her already. Donna would make a determined effort to be nice to the young woman.

When the server strolled to her table, Donna smiled. "Coffee, please. Tough day?" She angled her head in the direction of Sylvester and his bride-to-be.

"Yeah." She handed Donna a skinny menu. "Those two over there just got engaged." She practically spat the last word, but thankfully didn't. "She's too old for him."

"Oh?" Her eyebrows went up with the word. The server had more interest in the couple than an employee normally would.

"Oh, yeah."

A voice called from inside. "Danae!"

She hurried inside, leaving Donna curious. Danae must not like Linona, but it made her wonder why. Sure, Linona's family had money. Sometimes, that was enough. Often people resented those who drove better cars or lived in more expensive homes than they did. Her gaze drifted to the couple in question. Sylvester had his hair slicked back, looking like an actor in a foreign film. His unconstructed jacket and raw silk T-shirt were too cutting edge to fit into Legacy's conservative fashions.

In her opinion, he was trying too hard, but to someone like the young woman carrying her coffee, he could appear sophisticated. After all, the man wasn't from around here. He was the mysterious stranger.

"Here's your coffee." Danae placed the aromatic cup on the table.

"Thanks." The girl started back toward the shop as Donna wrestled with a way to keep her close. "I want to order."

Danae stopped and gave her a backward glance as if she'd misheard. She pivoted on the ball of her foot and passed by the happy couple, giving Sylvester a look of pure unadulterated longing. So, that's how it was.

"What do you want?" Her surly tone indicated she wasn't one to cry herself silly over a failed romance. She might even be the angry type.

"How's the crepe au Fromage de Chevre?"

"A soggy cheese pancake, that's how it is. Would you like to try again?"

Danae was making Donna regret any uncharitable thoughts she had about Tennyson and his melancholy attitude. "Your escargots?"

"They're snails. The only reason people eat them is because they made a mistake when they ordered them and aren't willing to admit they can't read French. Would you like me to bring you a croissant or a pastry? They have those shipped in from the bakery so they're okay."

Probably the same bakery she used when she didn't have time to bake. "That sounds wonderful. I trust your judgment." Build her trust to where she'd confide in her, although Donna didn't expect a relationship to blossom between them within the few minutes of interaction. If only she could insinuate she'd tip excessively well. That might make her server a little more loose-lipped.

A man dressed in a dark suit wandered out of the building and greeted Sylvester. "You're back!" The man threw up his hands and feigned surprise.

The newly engaged man jerked at the words and held up a hand as if to stop the chatty manager without any success.

"The famous chef from Sylvester's Salon in my humble café twice in one week."

Linona's voice pierced the pause. "Twice?"

"Ah, yes." The suited man bobbed his head. "Each time with a beautiful woman."

"I'm his fiancée." Linona pressed her left hand against her bosom, displaying her flashy engagement ring.

"My pardon," he said quickly. "It must have been his cousin. Yes, a cousin. I remarked on how much the two of you looked alike." Realizing he couldn't remedy the situation, the man promptly left.

Donna took a sip of her mediocre coffee and analyzed the scene she'd just witnessed. To the average person, it looked like a simple mistake. Not to her though, even though the man acted like it was an embarrassing error. The other woman had to have been J.E. If the manager disliked Sylvester for some reason, then it would explain his actions in revealing the meeting to Linona. Danae's yearning expressions had revealed her feelings to Donna, a complete stranger, but those who worked with the waitress knew her better. They'd also know if Danae and Sylvester had or were having a fling.

She held the cup up to her lips for another sip but it was slapped out of her hands, disrupting her train of thought. The liquid sloshed out of the cup onto her slacks, which made her grateful it was lukewarm as opposed to hot.

"Don't drink it." Mark's face loomed over hers. "You didn't drink any of it, did you?"

"A sip." Uniformed police officers milled around the tables. One took Linona and Sylvester's coffee cups, then poured the remaining liquid into evidence cylinders and labeled them. "Why couldn't you have just taken my cup as opposed to slapping it out of my hand?"

Mark reached for her coffee-soaked hand and gently dried it

with a napkin. "I couldn't take a chance. We need to get you to the hospital just to be sure. We traced the poison found in J.E.'s body to this café."

"How could you do that?"

Mark watched the uniformed cops come out of the restaurant with a struggling Danae between them and a protesting manager. Danae yanked a hand free and pointed at Sylvester. "I did it for you. She wouldn't have made you happy. Even though you trusted her, I knew she'd have written a deadly review. I saved your career. How could you throw me over for someone three times my age?"

Linona gasped, but Donna figured it was close to the truth.

"Take her away. I'll follow." Mark turned to respond to an officer who called his name, forcing Donna to grab onto his sports coat and tug, afraid he might leave before answering.

"You didn't tell me how you knew."

"The autopsy revealed the poison had been mixed with nutmeg-laced coffee. You mentioned the café, and it's the only place in town that puts nutmeg in their coffee. Most of the other places use cinnamon." He cupped her elbow and helped her to stand. "We're going to the hospital. Now!"

He gestured to Sylvester and Linona. "I suggest you two come to the hospital, too. It's better to be safe than wait until it's too late."

A WEEK HAD passed and her notoriety for helping solve a local murder had waned. The neighborhood book club even tendered her a new invite, which she refused by saying she was much too busy. Her mother had given up on matching her with a member of the silver set. Tennyson went back to wearing his shirts with cryptic sayings. Loralee ended up with Donna's mother, who insisted she was fostering the dog, not keeping it. Thank goodness, everything was back to normal. There were times when ordinary was underrated.

The super creepy guy who surprised her mother and her at Norelle's turned out to be the owner. Janice and he were at the talking stage. She swore the man had nothing to do with past-due meat served in New Orleans' restaurant mentioned in J.E.'s previous review. It was the former chef's fault. Donna made a mental note to avoid Norelle's in the future. It had been her experience that those who protest too much have something to hide.

Maria came in waving a newspaper. "You'll never believe what's in the paper."

She almost hated to ask but knew her sister-in-law would tell her anyhow. She might as well play along. "What's in the paper?"

The paper landed on the island countertop and slid a little. Maria had folded it to the article she wanted her to read. J.E.'s familiar banner topped half of the page with a small paragraph about the critic dying without mentioning how she died. "Well, so much for the plan to keep writing reviews using her name. The chain must have decided reporting her death would sell more papers."

"Possibly, all the chefs she lambasted probably bought a copy to be sure." Maria stabbed at the paper with a lacquered nail. "She had one last review. Keep reading!"

"There couldn't be a review. She didn't have a chance to go to any of the restaurants in Legacy." The trembling started in her hands, spread up to her arms and down her torso, forcing her to sit before she fell. "Noooo!"

"Okay." Maria snatched the paper. "I'll read it." She shook out the paper and cleared her throat. "Normally, this critic does not review any B and B's, but I happened across such a quaint one I had to mention it."

"Quaint. She might as well have said homely." Donna cradled her head in her hands. "Just when I thought we were getting ahead."

"Quaint isn't necessarily bad. It can mean charming, pretty, picturesque, and old-fashioned."

"Yeah, it also can mean peculiar, odd, and bizarre. How could she say much since about all we gave her was alcohol and toast?"

"Let me finish." She shook the paper. "'At The Painted Lady Inn service is paramount. The employees even dashed through the neighborhood to find the requested sherry. No matter how difficult the customer, service was never compromised. The inn is nestled in a quiet neighborhood in a sleepy coastal town.' Then it's more of the same. She calls the place cozy, too. It's an actual good review from someone who was known for her poison-pen reviews. People will remember the inn as the final good review."

"I guess there are times when having a critic at your inn can be a good thing. Though I'd prefer if the next one doesn't die."

Maria chuckled. "You and me both." She drifted toward the window and looked out. "I see Mark coming up the steps in a dark suit." She leaned close enough to the glass that she fogged it. "I think he got a haircut."

The bell on the door jangled as Mark let himself in. "Anyone home?"

Maria pointed to the back door and headed in that direction.

"In here," Donna called out, wondering what was wrong with her sister-in-law. At least she had left the paper.

The detective walked in the door, cradling dozens of flowers. Roses, lilies, gladiolas, carnations, even orchids bunched together, creating a scent bomb.

"Did you rob a florist?" A sense of expectation worked its way up her chest and settled in her throat like a partygoer who refuses to leave even after being shown the door.

The man chortled. "More like the florist robbed me. I didn't know what flowers you like so I got one of everything."

"Wow! What's the occasion?" She stood and worked her way over to the cabinet that held the vases. She could make several arrangements that would add charm to her quaint and cozy inn.

Mark placed the flowers on the counter and joined her at the cabinet where she peered into the back for extra vases. He placed his hands on her shoulders and gently turned her around. "When I saw you with that cup of possibly poisoned coffee to your lips, my heart stopped. I realized right then and there, I needed to let you know how important you are to me."

Donna rested her head against his chest. "You're not just saying that because I helped you solve another murder?"

"Well, I would hate to lose a great partner like you, almost as much as I despair of never eating your cheesecake."

"Just as I suspected."

The End

Janice's Critic-wowing Gazpacho Soup

Prepare a day in advance to allow the flavors to marinate in the fridge.

Ingredients

6 medium to large ripe tomatoes (preferably local), peel, chopped & diced around 6 cups.

1 medium red onion (diced)

1 cucumber (6-8 inches) peeled & diced

I sweet medium red bell pepper (orange, yellow or green can be used too) seeded & diced

2 stalks of celery (chopped) should equal one cup

1-2 Tbsp. Fresh parsley (chopped)

2 Tbsp. Fresh chives (chopped)

1 clove of garlic (minced) about 1 tsp

¼ cup red wine vinegar

¼-cup olive oil

1 Tbsp. freshly squeezed lemon juice

2 tsp. sugar or 2 stevia packets (depending on preference)

Salt and pepper to taste

6 or more drops of hot sauce to taste

1 tsp Worcestershire sauce (omit for vegan or vegetarian option)

2 cups tomato juice (or 1 15-ounce can crushed tomatoes if you don't have tomato juice)

Method

Place all ingredients in a large bowl. Use an immersion blender or a regular blender and blend in batches, to desired smoothness. Janice likes to leave it somewhat chunky to emphasize fresh veggies are present in this recipe.

Options

Add-ins include:

Chopped cilantro on the top

Fresh ground pepper

Sliced avocados on the top

Cold cooked shrimp on the top

Diced bacon on top

Don't use all of them at once. It would be a flavor overload. Chill overnight. Serves six.

Yummy Hot Ham & Cheese Rolls

Ingredients

1 can refrigerated pizza crust

¾ lb deli ham (thinly sliced)

12 slices of Swiss cheese (provolone or cheddar works too) thinly sliced

Glaze

½ cup (8 tbsp.) butter

2 tbsp. brown sugar

1 tbsp. Worcestershire sauce

1 tbsp. Dijon mustard

1 tbsp. poppy seeds

Directions:

*Preheat oven to 350 degree F. Liberally coat 9x13-inch rectangle pan with cooking spray.

*Unroll the pizza dough and shape into 9x13 rectangle.

*Top with ham, then cheese slices. Start rolling from the longer end similar to a jelly roll. Pinch seam together, flip the roll so the seam is down. Cut into one inch slices and place on prepared pan.

*Next combine the butter, brown sugar, Worcestershire sauce, mustard, and poppy seeds in a sauce pan over medium heat. Whisk the butter until it melts. When glaze is smooth, pour over the rolls.

*You can save for the next day or bake immediately.

*Bake uncovered for 25 minutes until golden brown.

Available Now

Christmas Calamity

By M. K. Scott

Chapter One

THE NINE-FOOT BLUE spruce wiped out an ornamental planter as Donna pushed at the cut trunk. The dull clunk of the concrete chunk explosion made her grit her teeth. Whose idea was it to have an old-fashioned Victorian Christmas? Oh yeah, right, hers. Her sister-in-law's voice penetrated the branches.

"Why did you stop pushing?"

A variety of answers crowded her head with number one being the stupid tree didn't fit. It had to fit. The front door boasted the largest clearance. There had to have been holiday celebrations in the inn in the past. Hard to imagine one without a stately decorated tree presiding over the festive event.

"Morning, Donna."

The greeting had her abandoning her hold on the fragrant trunk to wave to the dog walkers. "Good morning to you." Everyone would get to witness her very public battle with the evergreen. It also meant they'd witness her failure to push it through. The possibility had her grabbing the trunk, hoisting it up in a battering ram manner, and putting her weight behind it. The tree yielded under her weight and moved another foot until the wide bottom limbs caught on the door. The sound of a muttered complaint reached her.

"I wasn't ready. The vase you replaced that the guest took out almost needed another replacement." Maria's voice carried a tinge of weariness.

"Sorry."

Had Donna pushed her too hard getting ready for the season? Besides the inn, Maria had her regular job and a husband. Maria's burning goal had never been to run a Bed and Breakfast. Why did Donna expect everyone to have the same determination and unflagging stamina she did when it came to the inn? Lately, her endurance had flagged, and the prospect of an entire week off from both the inn and her job at the hospital held some attraction. A tropical cruise or just sunning on a white sand beach appealed. Toasted might be a better description since as a natural blonde, she only burned.

The cough of a wonky car motor accompanied her apology. The car slowed and turned into the inn parking lot. *What now?* Guests weren't to arrive for two more days. Any salesperson wanting to sell her everything from satellite television to pest control, she'd dealt with the first year of the inn opening, but there was a good chance with enough prompting from a supervisor they were ready to try again. *Please don't let it be a child selling something because she didn't feel very charitable.* Although, apple-cheeked scouts were seldom old enough to drive.

Tennyson, her sometime live-in helper, rounded the corner of the house. He stood on the lawn with his head cocked regarding Donna and the part of the tree she'd failed to ram through the door. "Looks like you need a hand."

"Yeah. I could probably use two or three hands." The sight of the young man relaxed her shoulders. The slender male may not have brawn on his side, but he was young. Instead of lending some muscle as she expected, he strolled around the tree, examining it from all angles before offering his opinion.

"Why didn't you get the mesh bag that compresses the limbs?"

Right now, she could see the reason behind such a device, but since leaving home her holiday history involved trees that came out of boxes where the color-coded limbs helped determine assembly. Maria shouted out an answer for her.

"Donna didn't want to pay the extra fifteen dollars for the bagging process! Thank goodness we had Daniel's truck. We'd never have been able to strap it to the car."

Even though it was the truth, it made her sound like Ebenezer Scrooge begrudging the poor a few pennies for their holiday. It was far from that. The tree farm people had a racket going. The tree itself was a hundred and twenty dollars. The white pine with the soft, lacy needles she intended to get was another forty dollars. Before she could come up with some comment about how it was highway robbery, another shopper had snapped up the white pine, leaving her to wrestle with the stubborn spruce.

Tennyson vanished for a few minutes and returned with a worn bed sheet. "Let's put the sheet under the tree and wrap it around the bottom branches. If we keep tension on the sheet, we should be able to get the tree inside."

Part of her wanted to make some comment about the viability of wrapping a tree up, but since she'd been making due with her tiny tabletop tree the last ten years, she kept her lips sealed. The two of them held the fabric taunt as Maria backed the tree into the foyer. *Success.*

Her fingers uncoiled their death grip on the sheet and were on the verge of letting go when Tennyson spoke. "We better hold onto the sheet until we get wherever you want the tree to go. Otherwise, the branches will explode out as if it was a green-hued ninja."

The colorful ninja would probably knock out a few things on the way, too. "The wedding parlor," she huffed out the words, even though Maria was already guiding the top of the tree in that direction. Despite the inclusion of the wedding chapel photos and information in both the brochure and website, so far, there'd been no takers for the chapel. Her sister-in-law thought if they staged a fake wedding complete with flowers and an attractive couple the idea would appeal to people more. Maria believed most couldn't see beyond the bare bridal arch and the molded white chairs.

Legacy hadn't earned its place as a destination wedding locale yet. That, combined with the fact fewer and fewer people were tying the knot, the chapel, so far, was a financial stumble. Still, she could use the space for events if she hid the arch in the storage room. This month it would represent a traditional Victorian Christmas or at least the Americanized fantasy. Her guests would not appreciate the lack of central heating or hot water to simulate the reality of olden days. They'd also probably nix brick dust to thicken their hot chocolate or chalk to whiten their milk. Nope, her guests would expect the tasty renditions of foods made on modern appliances with fresh spices as featured in holiday movies. Everyone knew how authentic movies were.

The three of them positioned the tree near the bay window after wrestling it into a tree stand. At night, the shimmering tree lights would be the perfect accent for her holiday decorating, at least from the outside. That reminded her that she needed to get the outside done, and she had an unexpected helper.

"Tennyson." She gave him a huge smile, but then tried to tone it down, realizing it would appear suspect. "I thought you went home to spend Christmas with your family."

Even though it would leave her shorthanded, even Donna wasn't Grinch enough to make someone work on Christmas. Only the hospitals, movie theaters, and restaurants did that.

"Yeah, that." He helped Maria move a table that looked awkward with the tree crowding it. Then the two of them tackled a few other items, making Donna wonder if he'd forgotten the question.

Eventually he stopped, wiping his sweaty brow and shrugged off his jacket. "I was hoping I could stay here and keep an eye on things so you could have a relaxing holiday."

The words all sounded good, almost too good. People always had a motive, good or bad, for their actions. Somehow she didn't think the male had her peace of mind entirely at heart. "That works. Not many guests. Of course, we still have old Saint Nick, who is working at the local mall, and the older couple, the Dickens, who came to spend the holidays with their newest grandchild."

Maria removed the white Chantilly lace tablecloths from the drum tables and replaced them with red ones. "Maybe their grandbaby is named Virginia or Snowflake."

Tennyson added with a grin, "Jack Frost or Tiny Tim."

"I doubt anyone would call their child Jack Frost, but I did go to high school with a girl named Merry Christmas. They spelled it the same, too. The poor girl hated her name. She couldn't do much about her last name, but her parents could have called her Teresa or Pamela."

Maria groaned. "Holly or Noel would have worked."

It made no sense to Donna, especially when people had nine months to pick out a name, and they still came up with horrible ones. Laney, from the maternity ward, would sometimes amuse them at lunch with some of the worst names.

"I'm sure she would have loved being called Holly Christmas. Her middle name could be Jolly." Maria snorted at the possibility.

"Since Tennyson is here, he can help me with the outside decorations. Maria, go home and get some rest."

"Appreciate it." Her sister-in-law gave her a salute and patted Tennyson's shoulder as she left the room.

The side door closing echoed through the house, proving Maria took Donna's suggestion seriously. Good. It wouldn't be a Holly Jolly Christmas if she ran her family ragged.

Tennyson half-turned in the direction of the hall door. "What's wrong with her? It's not even eleven, and she's tuckered." His gaze returned to Donna, who pulled on the tree, convinced it hadn't been centered in the window. "You're still going strong, and you're so much…"

His words trailed off once he realized he might insult his employer, the same person who was letting him hang out here because something was up at home.

"I'm so much what?" Donna knew he was going to say older. Not too surprising since her brother was younger and his wife even more so. In her opinion, Maria merited the label spring chicken since she wasn't even near forty.

"Ah, no, that wasn't it. I meant," Tennyson's eyes rolled up as he searched for a safe exit. Donna waited, suppressing the smirk that tugged at her lips. "Multi-talented," He finally muttered, ending the comment with a breathy sigh.

"I guess I am." She'd allow him that one, especially since she needed his help outside. "We can work on the parlor in the late afternoon. Let's get the outside done. We're having a Christmas Victorian Tea, and I have a special banner I need to stretch across the porch, along with the garlands, bows, and wreaths. I also have miles of fairy lights."

"What have I done?" Tennyson sagged against the wall, flung one arm over his eyes, and spoke in a stilted tone. "Woe is me."

The boy would never be an actor. Donna decided to needle him a little to see what would get a child out of the home over the holidays. Everyone knew that's when the best food happened, along with the Christmas specials and all the parties. "You could always go back home."

A spritely knock on the front door interrupted Tennyson's moan. Donna ambled to the door, knowing good and well it was unlocked. No reason for her few personal guests to knock. Everyone she wanted to see came through the back or side doors. Nothing good ever knocked. She stood in front of the door, debating whether to answer it. Whoever it was must have seen her through the narrow side windows beside the door.

A bearded man attired in a Victorian frock coat and hat stood on her front step. He nodded at her and glanced at a paper in his hand. "Mrs. Marley, I presume."

"You presume wrong."

The man glanced down at a slip of paper. "Ah, I see." He made a smart turn and headed down the street. Donna was tempted to watch and see what house he went to, but he kept walking. The shadows thrown by east side houses eventually swallowed him up.

Tennyson had followed her out in the hall. "Who was that?"

Weird. No one she recognized, that much she knew. Could be one of those costumed Christmas Carolers. That would be nice to have at the tea. Her hand, still on the doorknob, swung it open again, hoping to see the frock-coated man. The high-pitched yip of her neighbor's Yorkie rode the air, but no potential Christmas caroler.

"I don't know. Someone looking for the Marley home, I guess. He called me Mrs. Marley. Do you know anyone named Marley who lives in the neighborhood?"

"No, can't think of anyone, except…" He held up his index finger.

Donna turned expectant eyes on him. Teenagers often knew all the gossip, although they'd deny it. She knew Tennyson talked to some of them. An odd niggling sensation had settled in at the base of her neck at the peculiar visitor. "Who?"

"Jacob Marley. Ebenezer Scrooge's business partner."

"Really?" Donna rolled her eyes. Here she thought he'd say something pertinent. She gestured to the porch and pulled the door open. Tennyson followed, closing the door after him.

Two large cardboard boxes of fresh evergreen garlands waited on the front porch. A staple gun and a fluorescent tape measure sat on top of one box. She picked up the tape measure. "Here's the plan. We make six-foot garland loops and staple them onto the wooden porch railing. It has to be precise or someone in the neighborhood will tell me how I'm bringing the tone of the place down."

A cherry picker truck moved slowly down the street obviously looking for an address. It stopped a few houses past the inn. Two men wearing Elf hats hopped out. Tennyson pointed to the men who'd already knocked on the home owner's door and were chatting with the owner who was pointing to a ginormous evergreen in the front yard.

"They must be professional tree decorators." He nudged Donna and pointed again as if she hadn't gotten the message the first time. "That's what you need."

Yeah, she did. Donna needed the couple of thousand to pay the decorators, too. Some worked for as little as $1400, but that truck was bound to cost. "I got you. I'm set. Let's get to work."

Together they stretched the garland, measured it, stapled it, measured it again, and more often than not unstapled it and tried again. They worked quietly with the occasional *now* or *staple this*.

When she decided Tennyson had relaxed into his task, she queried him about his avoidance of home. "Soooo…" She stretched out the word and gave him a sideways glance. "…why decide to come back to work over the holidays?"

He gave her an irritated glance that almost made Donna laugh. Yeah, the kid was in a hard place. Since she was his employer, he couldn't blow her off the way he could a friend or relative. Tennyson could tell her it was personal and leave it at that. In her experience, when a noisy question was put out there, people answered. They realized, in hindsight, they didn't have to.

"Ah, it's awkward at home. Too many people and stuff." He shrugged and managed a lopsided grimace.

No wonder he came back to the inn for sanctuary. Tennyson had never struck her as a party animal. The chaos, noise, and the people alone would send him fleeing, but an old girlfriend who hung around had to be super awkward. She stapled the last bit of garland to the edge of the railing. No way she'd discuss personal issues with someone young enough to be her son.

"Not an issue for me. As an adult, I have control of my own life. I call the shots."

The soft purr of a well-tuned engine moved closer and stopped in front of the inn. Before she could look, Tennyson announced the visitor.

"Oh look, it's your mother."

Donna closed her eyes. Too late to recall her last statement.

Author Notes

> If you enjoyed this book, try checking out Murder Manion, book one in the series, and Drop Dead Handsome, book two in the series.

> Write a review.

> Do you have an idea for a story or a character name? Love to hear it. I can be reached through my website www.morgankwyatt.com

> Want to get free books, read excerpts before everyone else, receive special members only swag and giveaways? You need to be on the mailing list. Go over to my website and sign up. (I don't sell my mailing list and guard it as well as I do my chocolate.)

> Do you like humor with your suspense? Check out **Suspicious Circumstances: He Loves Me Not.**

> Love to meet you, check out my personal appearances on the website too.

> Can you do one more thing? Go out and have an amazing day.

M. K. Scott

Printed in the USA
CPSIA information can be obtained
at www.ICGtesting.com
LVHW091132290923
759703LV00019B/151